I, SPY

A BLETCHLEY PARK MYSTERY

RHIAN TRACEY

Piccadilly
PRESS

First published in Great Britain in 2023 by
PICCADILLY PRESS
4th Floor, Victoria House, Bloomsbury Square
London WC1B 4DA
Owned by Bonnier Books, Sveavägen 56, Stockholm, Sweden
www.piccadillypress.co.uk

A CIP catalogue record for this book is available from the British Library.

ISBN: 978-1-80078-440-6
Also available as an ebook

1

This book is typeset using Atomik ePublisher
Printed and bound in Great Britain by Clays Ltd, Elcograf S.p.A.

Piccadilly Press is an imprint of Bonnier Books UK
www.bonnierbooks.co.uk

I, SPY

This book is dedicated to my great-aunt Audrey Mary Lewis (née Letton), whose remarkable time at Bletchley Park, as a codebreaker, inspired this story. And for the people who served during the war, those we know about and those we don't – thank you for your service.

History, despite its wrenching pain, cannot be unlived,
but if faced with courage, need not be lived again.

Maya Angelou

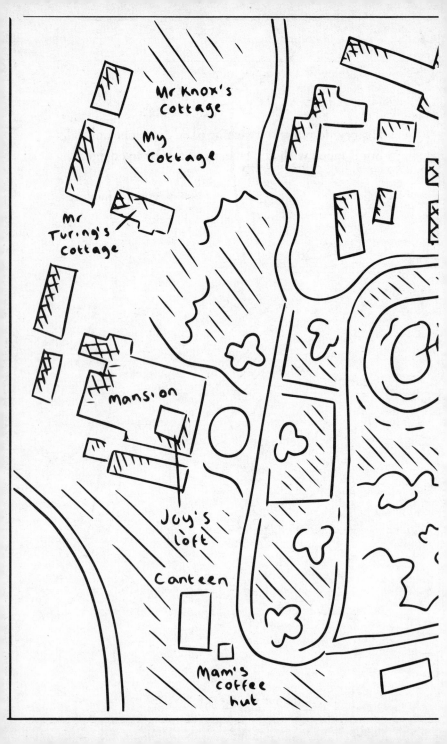

1

Late September 1939

Gunshots rang out across the parkland and Robyn slipped from a high branch of the willow tree, just managing to grab on to a lower one; the bark was coated in slimy green lichen. She'd climbed up to get a better look – something was happening at the Mansion. A blast pulsed through the air as she dug her nails into the bark to avoid sliding further.

From her vantage point up the tree on the island she'd watched steady streams of men in forces uniform arrive at the park. A new eight-foot fence, topped with barbed wire, framed the perimeter of the estate, but the tree's roots would snake under the fence no matter how high and wide they built it. Trees couldn't be locked out – the keys were in the seeds.

She thought about her favourite: the spiny seedpods that dropped from horse-chestnut trees and cracked open when ripe to reveal all the potential future trees inside; a war couldn't stop *them*. Even though the war had, technically, started a few weeks ago, guards had appeared at the front and back gates first thing this morning, as if the enemy might descend on them at any moment. They hadn't stationed guards by the side gates at the end of the woods or by St Mary's Church, at least not yet, but Bletchley Park was starting to look like a prison, rather than her home. Another thunderous explosion sent her tumbling from the lowest branch. Even though she knew it was Mr Maelor testing equipment with the men in the stables, it felt far too real.

Cat-like, she landed on all fours, her hands resting on the ground confettied with leaves. The hairy white fingers of the willow mixed with the waxy glossy-green leaves of the beech. She jumped up and ran across the small island to where she had tied up her boat. Her breath ballooned in the cool morning air, a puffball of vapours. Robyn hopped into her boat, took up the oars and rowed swiftly back across the lake. Her father would be furious if he caught her out here. Mr Maelor and the men who had taken over the stables weren't just making a racket to pass the time; they were practising their defences. Her father *had* told her to stay away from the island, but it had slipped her mind, what with the excitement of the forces turning up!

As she rowed, the gunshots suddenly fell silent. She could hear the buzzing of darting billy witch bugs and other insects again. A chevron of Canada geese croaked out repetitive comeback calls as they returned from their dawn raids in the fields. They landed in a tightly knit V formation on the lawn, looking like a regiment of soldiers. Watching the animals' daily routines made Robyn feel steady and safe. Whatever was going on in the war, and here at Bletchley Park, the geese were completely oblivious to it.

Robyn tied up her boat at the landing stage, hoping it wouldn't be the last time she'd be able to use it. Last night, her parents had put new rules in place. No *more rowing on the lake. No more bothering with the birds – and heaven help her if she were to try to bring any more wounded animals home. And no more swimming out to the island.* Might as well make up a rule to forbid her from having any more fun. Each day a little more freedom evaporated, and the park felt . . . strange, like somewhere she *used* to know.

She sprinted across the dewy lawn, sliding to a stop as military vehicles shook and shuddered their way up the drive. She could see her father from a distance, directing traffic. He'd been organising his garages, deciding which vehicles should go where. Of course, he'd told her none of this. She'd been following him for weeks, across the courtyard from their cottage to the garages. He'd told her that he wasn't the chauffeur any longer, but Head of Transport, and either his clipboard or his little black notebook seemed to be in his hand. A shot shattered the silence, far too close for comfort. Robyn looked up then covered her head instinctively. A pigeon burst from the sky, flying towards the Mansion roof at speed, its wings beating fast. It must have spotted a crack in the eaves and was looking for a place to hide; she couldn't blame it. She dropped to the ground, which was vibrating, sending pins and needles through her palms.

3

When it fell quiet, she got to her feet and ran as fast as she could back to the cottage. Change knotted itself around her throat, like one of the itchy scarves her mother insisted Robyn wore because of her *bad chest*. As far as she was concerned, she didn't have a bad chest, she was positively bursting with health! Her mother spent far too much time listening to episodes of *The Radio Doctor*. But Robyn had to admit, if only to herself, that her mother had been right. Everything would be different after today. The war – *the real war* – had arrived at their door, bringing with it enough danger to burn the whole house down. At least, that's what her father had said last night when he thought she was asleep. She made many interesting discoveries while sitting at the top of the stairs, in the dark.

The smart-looking convoy halted outside the Mansion. Robyn paused in the red-brick passageway between the two cottages to watch. Doors opened. People stepped out, their sensible shiny shoes crunching on the pebbles. She divided the strangers by their different-coloured uniforms. Their stripes spoke of rank and importance. Their purposeful chatter filled the air. Robyn's heart beat faster as she ran to the back door and booted it open, narrowly missing the milk bottles lined up on the step. The blue tits had been thieving again. The feathery crooks had drilled tiny holes through the foil with their beaks, siphoning off the fat-rich cream from the top of the bottle. The smell of tea and damp clothes drying enveloped her as she stepped into the kitchen.

'Oh, Robyn! Look at your boots,' her mother said, spinning around from the sink. 'Completely caked in duck muck. And they've only just come back from the repair shop.'

4

'Sorry,' she said uselessly, dropping her sketch book onto the kitchen table.

She started emptying her pockets of the pine cones and conkers she'd collected; she'd managed to find a massive conker, still cloaked in its spiky case, which looked like an armoured snail shell. There would be plenty of conkers tournaments at school now it was autumn, and this one was sure to beat anything Mary could find. The park boasted the best horse chestnut trees in Bletchley. Her father had told her that horse chestnuts could live for almost three hundred years; she wondered how old the ones at the park were.

'You can clean your boots after,' her mother said. 'Sit down and eat your bread and jam . . . oh, and wait until your father gets in. He's got something to tell you. And stop polishing those conkers! If you've a mind to polish, there's plenty of dusting to be done.'

She was only allowed to bring the conkers into the cottage because her mother said they kept the spiders away. She didn't think this was true at all, but if it meant she could bring more of the outside inside, she didn't mind. Several pots of homemade jam were laid out on the table, but Robyn had lost her appetite. She always dreaded the words *wait until your father gets in*.

'You'll need to wash your hair tonight, mind. Thank goodness I cut it into a Princess Elizabeth bob; at least we'll not be waiting all night by the fire for it to dry any more.'

A few days ago her mother had *set to* with the kitchen scissors, chopping Robyn's hair. A black-and-white photograph of Princess Elizabeth's neat bob guided her mother as she hacked at Robyn's long chestnut waves. Mary's shocked face at school the next day had told Robyn all she needed to know about her new look.

'They want to see you up in the big house,' her mother said now.

Her mother called it the big house and some of the children at school called it the madhouse, but everyone else called it the Mansion. Rumours had spread that Bletchley Park was going to be an asylum for the mentally ill. She'd tried to deny it, but no one wanted to listen to the boring truth, especially from her, *the chauffeur's daughter.*

'Why? What do they want to see *me* for?' she panicked. 'I haven't done anything!'

'Hush, Robyn, the ladies next door are doing important work with Mr Knox. Keep your voice down,' her mother warned. She was already the ladies' number-one fan.

The ladies were unusual for women at the park because they didn't work with the other typists and administrators in the Mansion. Instead, they were closeted in Mr Knox's cottage. Robyn wasn't sure what they were working on, but they most definitely weren't typing up letters for grand-looking men in suits and uniform. They even had a nickname – Dilly's Fillies, which made Robyn screw up her nose and feel wriggly.

Her mother had started sending her next door with batches of Welsh cakes. They were firm favourites with the lady who always wore a bow tie, and had a bob, but carried it off with far more grace and style than Robyn could ever hope to muster.

Her mother cracked an egg against the mixing bowl. Robyn watched, transfixed, as the clear fluid slipped from the shell. Two balls of sunshine. The double-yolker plopped into the base of the bowl, breaking her trance.

'Am I not going to school today, then?' she asked hopefully. School was dull as ditchwater. She'd far rather stay at home with her father and tinker with engines and cars in the garages.

'No,' her mother confirmed. 'You're not going back to school at all. In fact, you're to stay put here for now. No more wandering off into the woods, or down to the river or . . . anywhere. Are you listening? Do you understand me? You're not to go off site at all, Robyn. I'm serious, mind.'

'What? Why not?' Robyn sat up in excitement. 'And what do you mean *off site*? You're talking strangely, Mam. We've got nature day coming up and my birthday soon and Mary and I are going to try out our new conkers tomorrow. I can't not go to school! Don't be silly!' She tried to laugh, but looking at her mother's face, she wondered if she was serious.

She had thought she'd be stuck at school until she turned fourteen, which wasn't for another whole long year. They weren't going to let her leave early, were they? Or had her father given in? Was he finally going to let her join the other apprentices in the garages? She'd be the youngest. And the first girl. She wasn't sure that it was even allowed, but who cared! She'd work ten times harder than all the boys in there. If her father gave her a chance, she'd be the best mechanic he'd ever taken on.

'Sit still a minute. Your father will go up to the big house with you tomorrow.'

'Am I not going back to school *ever*, then?'

'I don't know, do I? Stop asking so many questions. Your father will tell you. He should have taken you in there by now. They wanted to see you before today, but he's been that busy with the new operation . . .' Her mother stopped herself.

'Busy with *what*? What new operation?' she tried. But her mother was back on red alert, lips sealed and all secrets locked down.

It seemed this new operation might involve her and then she'd find out what *things* were going on in the garages. That must be why they'd decided to take her out of school. It all made sense if you thought about it. And all the better if she was allowed to start her apprenticeship as a mechanic slightly early. Maybe her father was waiting until her birthday to ask her. Or maybe he'd tell her during her first driving lesson with him. That would be the best birthday present ever!

'So, that's why I'm not going back to school – this new *operation* with Dad?'

'Never you mind,' her mother said. 'Eat up. Then clean your boots, see to the hens and after that I've got a long list of jobs to keep you busy until your father gets home.'

Robyn stifled a groan at the prospect of one of her mother's dreaded *lists*, but she bubbled with excitement at knowing her father was going to share a secret with her. Later, she'd find a way to sneak down to school at going-home time and let Mary know what was happening. Not that she had many details to share with her best friend. But if she didn't tell someone that her boring school days were over and her real life was about to begin, she'd burst.

2

Pine cones dropped around her like grenades before being carried off by scavenging squirrels, while wood pigeons methodically stripped the trees of their autumn leaves. The clock house chimed three as Robyn pulled her bicycle out of the plum shed where she'd shoved it and had a quick look at the tyres. The front one was as thin and flat as a pancake. She could change a puncture no bother, but she'd have to sneak back inside to get her puncture kit from the scullery. And she couldn't do that without her mother spotting her. She shoved the useless bicycle back in the shed. She'd have to leg it if she wanted to catch Mary before she headed back to her digs at horrid Mrs Fisher's. Mary's evacuee digs were dreadful, but until there was a better offer she was stuck living with miserable Mrs Fisher and her whiny children.

Robyn looked around before setting off across the lawn in front of the Mansion at a run. People marched across the gravelled drive, folders and papers under their arms.

She noticed that what she'd thought was a shelter and had been empty earlier was now full of black bicycles. There must be at least twenty or so lined up in there. Whose were they and why were there so many of them?

They'd never had a bicycle shed at the park before. Mary would have spotted it, as she kept a close eye on things. Slowing down to a casual jog, Robyn made her way over. They were all adult bicycles, apart from one green one at the end.

Even though it was smaller than the rest it would still be a stretch for her, and there was no one around to ask if she could borrow it. All the same, she pulled it out and climbed on. When she put her feet on the ground and tested the brakes they seemed to work. She checked the white tyres. Both were plump and pumped.

Robyn set off on the path towards the woods then slammed on the brakes. She pulled her satchel off and placed it in the wicker basket on the front of the bicycle. *That's better. I look like I'm off to work or taking something important to someone somewhere – which I am.*

Mary was the most important person in her life. There was no way Robyn was going to leave school at the drop of a hat and not let her best friend know. But a worst-case scenario had kept her awake last night: Mary might be sent back home to Liverpool at any moment. Robyn didn't even have her address. They weren't supposed to share things like that any more because . . . *There's a war on, don't you know?* She had heard that so often since the prime minister had announced, at the beginning of the month, that, 'This country is at war with Germany.'

10

The green bicycle wasn't too bad. It was much easier to balance with her heavy satchel in the wicker basket. Inside was a book she had to return to Mary. She hadn't read it, but she didn't want to steal it by accident, and it might be difficult for them to meet up from now on.

Robyn bumped across the uneven pathways of the woods, taking care not to hit any tree roots. She didn't have time to fall off or damage a bicycle that wasn't hers. There were several logs piled up in the undergrowth. Someone must have been in the woods felling trees, which seemed a bit odd. She stopped and peered through a set of padlocked wrought-iron gates, into a graveyard. The coast was clear. There was enough room to squeeze between the wall and the gate on the left and pull the bicycle through behind her. She freewheeled down the lane to school, hands off the green bars, enjoying the wind in her short hair. She'd regret that later when she tried to get a comb through the knots, but for now if felt like she was flying.

School was in sight. Most people had already left, apart from a few boys still kicking a football around the yard. She screeched to a halt and her satchel catapulted out of the basket and landed by the gate. Coins scattered on the ground. She threw the bicycle down and dashed to pick them up. She'd meant to hide her subs money but had forgotten to empty her bag. The profits from her Bird and Tree club were growing. One day she was going to buy a car. Her father had promised he'd help her find an old one and they'd work on it together. And his present for her thirteenth birthday was to be her very first driving lesson!

'Owen! Oi! Owen? Have you seen Mary?' Robyn shouted

at one of the boys playing football. She picked up the last of her coins and shoved them back in her satchel.

'Gone home,' Owen said. 'We doing Bird and Tree club today, then, or what?'

'Nah, I haven't got time. Next week.'

She wasn't that keen on Owen being part of her club. He didn't take the bird-spotting part seriously and he couldn't draw for toffee. He was in it for larking about and being the first to climb to the top of the tallest tree. But she couldn't turn down his money and he always brought some of his friends, so she tolerated him.

'She hasn't gone home. She's gone for special lessons. *Extra* lessons,' Thomas said meaningfully, as if Robyn should have known what her best friend was up to.

But this was the first time she had heard about it. She ran over and asked the boys, 'Special lessons? With who? What for?'

'Dunno. Prob'ly going to do posh exams or go to university, or something. She's such a boffin. Mr Alquin's pet, ain't she?' Thomas sniffed, wiping his nose on the back of his hand.

'Girls can't go to university, you idiot!' Owen said, tackling Thomas and taking the ball.

'Shows what you know, Owen James,' Robyn retorted. 'My Aunt Kate went to Oxford and my Aunt Eleri went to Cambridge, so there. And if anyone is going to go to university, it'll be Mary and not you.'

'Don't care!' Owen ended the conversation by booting the ball against the wall.

Except he did care, because Owen had been top of the class before Mary arrived. Robyn wasn't going to get anything else out of Owen and Thomas, as they were now arguing about the offside rule. There wasn't time to cycle to Mrs Fisher's either; not if she wanted to get back before her mother noticed she'd disappeared. She could write a note and leave it in Mary's tray in the classroom, but what would she say? Besides, she didn't have a pencil or paper, just her sketch book and Mary's book, and she didn't want to rip a page from either of those; although Robyn would never understand why, Mary's library books were precious to her. She'd have to come back tomorrow. And much earlier, if she wanted to catch Mary, in case she was going to sneak off for more special lessons with Mr Alquin. She and Mary told each other everything, or so she'd thought. Never mind, she'd find out about it tomorrow. It must have slipped Mary's mind, that was all.

'Oi! Have you got any spare jam jars for nature day tomorrow?' Owen shouted as she got back on her bicycle. 'We haven't got any and my mum says your mum will have loads, the amount of hedge jam she makes. Can I borrow some? I want to catch a frog or a toad.'

'Or an eel!' Thomas added.

'You won't fit an eel in a jam jar. Anyway, I don't know if I'll be in school tomorrow.'

She'd been looking forward to nature day for weeks and now she was going to miss it! Mr Alquin had promised that she could lead part of the lesson on bird-spotting. She'd been practising her talk to the ducks, who were a receptive audience and only heckled a bit. And now it would all go to waste.

'You don't look poorly.' Thomas picked up the football and held it under his arm while he stared at Robyn. 'You're red in the face. And very sweaty,' he added helpfully.

'Got to go!' she shouted over her shoulder, readying herself to cycle back up the hill.

She squeezed through the gap between the ivy-covered wall and the gates. Thomas was right, she was hot and cross and must look a sight.

She didn't expect to find a guard there.

'And where do you think you're going?' he demanded. 'You've never stolen a Park bicycle too, have you? Blimey, young lady, you *are* in trouble. Mr D will want to see you.'

Mr D, also known as the Commander, oversaw all operations at Bletchley Park. Essentially, he was her father's boss. The very last person you'd want to be in trouble with.

'You'd better come with me,' said the guard and spun around, setting off at a pace towards the Mansion.

3

'Enter!' a voice beckoned from behind the heavy wooden door.

Robyn felt a bit queasy as the guard hissed, 'In you go,' under his breath before stepping aside. It reminded her of being summoned to Mrs Ashman's study at school. With a sinking feeling in her stomach as she mentally listed all the possible reasons she could have been called to see the headmistress. She supposed Mr D was like the headmaster here, in charge of everyone and everything and always the cleverest person in the room. Her father, who called the Commander 'a genius', had once done an impression of him at the kitchen table for her mother, making himself look broader by puffing out his chest and taking on a gentle Scottish accent as he pretended to swing a golf club and called out, 'Fore!'

An elegant bay window filled the small room with light. A deep-brown wooden desk dominated the room while a smaller one was set off in a recess to the side. A grand-looking coat, hat and umbrella stand stood to the right. Behind the large desk sat a very tall, slender man; not at all what she'd expected. Although the room was fine, she'd have thought that Mr D's office would be bigger too, and more suitable for a commander.

Mr D was writing something on a piece of paper with a smart fountain pen. A woman sitting at the smaller desk was watching Robyn. The door shut behind her, and she was trapped with nowhere to run or hide. She stood in front of the large desk, wondering if all this fuss was really over a borrowed bicycle. She raised her chin and pulled back her shoulders.

'Miss Hughes, read out the charges, if you would,' the man instructed without pausing to stop or look up at her. He didn't have a Scottish accent and he wasn't wearing naval uniform, though she was certain her father had said the Commander was in the Navy.

'Theft of park property. Going off site without permission. Returning to site without signing in at the sentry gates or showing a pass. And speaking to civilians in a suspect manner,' Miss Hughes said officiously.

'And how do you plead, young lady?' The tall man finally stopped writing and adjusted his glasses to look at her as if he were a judge in a courtroom.

Robyn quickly began her defence. 'How am I supposed to show a pass? I live here, don't I? And I didn't steal anything. I only borrowed the bicycle because mine had a flat. I was on my way to put it back. There were loads of bicycles there, I didn't think anyone would mind . . .' Then she ran out of breath.

'And there we have it, Miss Hughes. She *didn't think*.' The man tutted, placing Robyn's satchel on his desk. The guard had taken it from her and must have given it to him.

'Take notes, please, Miss Hughes!' he ordered.

'Yes, sir,' Miss Hughes agreed, as if Robyn were a dangerous criminal.

'And these civilians you were consorting with –' the man began.

'It's only Owen and Thomas!' she interrupted. '*They're* not civilians. They're boys. I asked them where my friend was, but they didn't know.' Her skin tingled as if it was being stroked by stinging nettles. Who had been watching her and why?

'A likely story. And this is the satchel you were using to transport items off site?' the thin man accused. 'What were you delivering?'

'Nothing! I wasn't delivering anything, I'm hardly a dispatch rider!' she joked. But her unnatural laugh echoed awkwardly in the silent room.

'Wipe that smirk off your face!' The man stood up, grabbed the satchel and spilt its contents onto the patterned carpet.

'*No!* Those are my things!' Robyn dropped to the floor to pick up her money, her sketch book and Mary's book.

'Stop right there!' the man commanded, holding up one of his leather-gloved hands. 'Don't move an inch. Miss Hughes, collect those coins and papers and bring them to me. I need to inspect any incriminating evidence.'

Miss Hughes stopped taking notes and came over. She picked the items up off the floor and placed them on the desk.

'Money, hmm. What were they paying her for?' he asked Miss Hughes.

'It's mine!' Robyn protested as he gathered the coins together and set them to one side, his attention drawn by her sketch book. This man couldn't take her things, could he?

'Indeed. And how, I wonder, does a girl like you get quite so much money?'

'I earned it,' she said.

He might not believe her if she told him about the Bird and Tree club. To be honest, she wasn't sure she should be taking money off her classmates, but she wanted that car.

'And these drawings? Why do you have so many of them?' He passed her sketch book to Miss Hughes.

She had to stop herself from cannonballing across his desk to grab her sketch book from his spindly fingers.

'They're birds. I like drawing them.' She shrugged. This was silly – they really were just sketches of the island and the animals and plants at the park.

'And why do you have these? Engines and vehicles.' He stalked behind her, as if he were a police officer questioning her in an interview room.

'Oh.' She'd forgotten about those; she knew she wasn't supposed to be in the garages any more. Her father had told her so without giving her a good reason why. 'They're bits and bobs from Dad's garage. New cars that come in and other ones that we fix up together. Or used to . . . I'm not allowed in there now. I used to draw what they looked like before and after, but I don't go in there.' She crossed her fingers behind her back. 'Where is my dad? *I want my dad*,' she said under her breath.

'Oh, don't you worry. I will be speaking to your father about all this.' He waved at her pictures, the coins and Mary's book still lying on the floor.

'And what do we have here?' he asked as he bent down to pick it up before flicking through the pages.

'My friend's book. I was going to give it back, but she wasn't there.'

Robyn was relieved he'd stopped looking through her sketch book. But was she going to get Mary involved in whatever all *this* was?

'Are these letters?' He held out a circular scrap of paper.

'It's our language.' She shrugged. 'It's just a game.'

It had been Mary's idea to come up with their own language using two different letter wheels. It meant they could send notes that would look like nonsense to anyone else.

'What language? A code!' He looked sharply at Miss Hughes, who raised her neat eyebrows at him.

'Yes, so we can pass notes in class,' Robyn said.

She bunched her hands into fists at her sides to stop them shaking. They weren't supposed to write notes in class. Mr Alquin would be so disappointed in them both if he found out.

'File these, Miss Hughes, until we can decipher them,' he ordered.

'Yes, sir,' Miss Hughes replied, with an air of concern.

Robyn wished Miss Hughes would address the man by his name so she could remember it. Because if this wasn't Mr D, then who was he?

'Were you given permission to leave site?' The man put his hands behind his back and began pacing. He was starting to scare her.

'No,' she faltered. Her legs felt funny, as if she'd been standing up for too long.

'Do you not understand simple rules? Are you not able to do as you're told, miss?' he spat at her.

'Yes! I'm not stupid!' She tried to defend herself, but her voice wobbled and cracked, giving away how upset she was.

'And yet, here we are.' He gestured around the room. 'I will be keeping these papers and this book. Miss Hughes will examine them and then I will speak to your father to see how we will proceed in this matter. Dismissed!'

'Can I have my satchel back?' she asked. 'And my sketch book?' She didn't really care about the bag, but her drawings were another matter.

'Don't be ridiculous. Miss Hughes, show her out and bring me her father. Immediately!' the man ordered, picking up his pen and returning to his work.

4

As her father guided her under the arch, into the formal foyer of the Mansion, a barrage of noise greeted them. She'd always wanted to enter the Mansion but until yesterday she never had. She'd tried to sneak inside a few times, but one of the officious-looking men in uniform always stopped her. Last week, she'd made it as far as the kitchens before a chef in whites shooed her away, like a cat begging for scraps. The guard who'd caught her with the borrowed bicycle yesterday had escorted her in through the back, so she'd never been through the front before now. A second set of doors led into a dark wood-panelled hallway with a series of rooms opening off it.

Her father entered one of the rooms, whispering to her that he needed to speak to someone. As she followed him, she wondered how many times he had been inside the Mansion. Considering he worked down in the garages, he looked very much at home and seemed to know lots of people here. Maybe this was where he'd been spending most of his time recently, instead of walking around the lake with her, or looking for tracks in the woods, or teaching her about all the varied species of plants at the park.

He didn't make time for her any more and she missed him. He even came home too late to go on their stargaze strolls, as he liked to call them. Apparently his father had taken him on them when he was a boy. They'd started their late night stargazing walks when she'd turned ten, much against her mother's wishes.

She wondered again what the tall thin man had said to her father to make him so furious with her last night. Her mother hadn't even spoken to her over breakfast this morning. The silent treatment was far worse than any shouting. At least with shouting it was over with and you knew where you stood.

Blackout curtains cloaked the large drawing room in gloom and, despite several lamps scattered about, it was still dark. Windows crisscrossed with brown tape made the space feel enclosed. Typewriters clattered and printers spat out long jagged sheets, punched with holes, that looked like paper snowflakes. Smart-looking women wearing headsets picked up the strips and marched off into the corridor with them.

The women looked clever, and they wore pressed shirts, navy skirts and heels. Most of them had applied mascara and a dash of bold red lipstick. Their floral perfume mingled with the smell of freshly roasted coffee brewing.

Terribly glamorous, Robyn thought, looking down at her school uniform in dismay. Her mother had done her best to make Robyn presentable but somehow she always ended up looking scruffy.

She didn't know where these stylish women were taking the papers or why, but they held them carefully, as if they were extremely important. Robyn wished she could follow the women. And read what was on those sheets.

A rainbow of telephones sat on evenly spaced desks. There were black, green and even red sets, though she'd had no idea telephones came in any colour other than black. The red ones looked dramatic. Robyn was fighting the urge to reach out and pick up the receiver closest to her when her father reappeared by her side and tipped his head down to hers. His coarse whiskers brushed against her ear. She strained to hear him over the clicketty-clack of typing.

'We're to go upstairs. Remember what I said: tell the truth.'

She followed him out of the room towards a grand staircase next to a set of open double doors leading to a ballroom. Robyn wanted to run into the room and slide across the floor on her knees, but her father grabbed her arm.

'Answer their questions. And then keep your head down until they forget about you.'

She nodded, keeping her eyes on her feet as they climbed, so she wouldn't trip or tread mud into the thick burgundy carpet. At the top of the staircase they came to a pair of closed doors. She spied a further set of uncarpeted stairs leading upwards, but her father took her hand and led her along a gallery lined with dark and gloomy paintings in thick dull frames that looked so heavy they might topple off the wall. The gallery reminded her of the last time she and her mother had gone up to London to see the sights. Her mother had dragged her around a desperately boring museum to stare at enormous paintings of every king and queen that had ever sat on a throne. Robyn sighed at the memory; what a waste of her last trip to the city. There'd be no more visits there now.

'Here we are,' her father said, nudging her through an open door. 'In we go, Birdy.' But a uniformed guard shook his head and blocked her father's way.

'No need. You've already signed,' he told her father.

'But she's just a child. She's my daughter. Surely I should . . .' her father began.

'No need. She'll be done soon enough,' the man said firmly, his arm still blocking the doorway.

'I'll be right outside, Birdy,' her father tried to reassure her as the door clicked shut in his face.

Why hadn't they let him come in with her? Robyn really was on her own.

She looked around to work out what this was all about. The room was square. There was a small fireplace, a few wooden chairs and a long table draped with an itchy-looking grey blanket. Three men, all without a hair out of place, sat behind the table in silence. She recognised the different uniforms: Army on the left and Navy on the right. And in the middle was the tall spindly man from the interrogation in the study.

'Sit down; we have a few questions we'd like to ask you,' said the thin man, gesturing to a chair.

'Name, please?' He hunched his shoulders, bending over a notebook in front of him.

Oh, so he wanted to exchange pleasantries today, did he? He hadn't been very polite yesterday. Maybe he'd be different in front of these forces men. How two-faced. And highly suspect.

'Name!' he said again, more impatiently this time. His veil of manners was slipping already.

'Robyn Audrey Lewis,' she replied as if she were at school.

Which she ought to be. By the river with her friends and their jam jars, trying to catch specimens to study. Mary must have partnered with someone else. *Who?* Robyn wondered unhappily.

'Age?' he continued, without looking at her.

She had more time to observe him this morning. A slick black strip ran along his parting, dividing the rest of his greying hair.

'Twelve. Nearly thirteen.' She sat up straighter in the chair, trying out her best smile on the men. 'It's my birthday next month.' She smiled wider, thinking about the driving lessons with her father.

There was no response. Robyn tucked her hands underneath her legs. She wouldn't let the men see them shaking. She wished her parents had told her what this was all about, but they never told her anything these days!

'Address?' the man in the suit carried on.

'Number 2 Cottage, Bletchley Park,' she answered, stifling a sigh; this was a bit dull.

They'd always called their house *the* cottage, but now

there were Mr Knox and the ladies next door at number three. And there were some serious-looking men working in the bungalow opposite. So someone had numbered the cottages and theirs was now number two.

'You walk to school, correct?' The man in the suit spoke with authority.

'Yes, that's right. Church Green Road,' she replied.

'And at school, do the other children ask you questions? Those boys from yesterday, what were they asking you about?' he prompted.

'I've already told you.'

'Did they ask you about here? Do the children at school ask you what's going on here, at the park?' he barked.

A salt-and-pepper beard concealed the lower half of his face, the hairs springing up around his lips like moss. He was still wearing the brown leather gloves.

'Well, yes.' She knew better than to lie, but their reaction made her wince.

The man's long neck snapped up and the other two men sat forward in their chairs. *That was it!* He'd reminded her of a bird, and now she knew which one: a heron.

'*And?* What do they ask you?' The heron-man's face changed; he looked excited.

Now she'd made the connection she couldn't see anything *but* a heron staring back at her. The Heron looked eager, as if he couldn't wait for her to answer, his jaw jutting forward.

'Look, you're not in trouble, all right,' the Army man said. 'We just need to know who paid you and what you told them.'

'They only paid me because I set up a club. I teach them

how to climb. Half of them are useless at it and would break their arms and legs if I wasn't there. And I show them how to be quiet and spot things, as if they're in a hide.'

'Spot what things? Why are you hiding? And who are you spying for?' the Heron demanded.

'No one. It's not spying! Its bird-spotting,' she laughed. 'And when they ask me what happens here, I say it's about the war effort: secretaries and typewriters. Dull as ditchwater, I tell them; nothing exciting at all.'

The truth was she didn't know what was going on at Bletchley Park because no one told her anything. But that hadn't stopped her spinning out a few tall tales at school. When Mary had first arrived it had been raining and they'd all huddled in the cloakroom and Mary got out her tin of evacuee chocolates and raisins to share. Sarah-Ann, Kim, Lily and Ruby had quizzed Mary, interested in the new girl. Robyn could tell Mary didn't like the attention, so she had made something up about the park. Something dangerous. She exaggerated the rumours about the madhouse, until Mary's evacuee experience was as interesting as yesterday's fish-and-chip paper. But Robyn wasn't going to share *that* story with these men.

'And they believed you?' the Navy man clarified. 'The children at school?' His chair creaked as he leant forward. When she nodded, he looked suspicious.

'What about adults? Does anyone stop and ask you any questions?' The Heron took over again. He picked up his plain trilby hat, turning it in his hand by the brim as he waited for her response.

'No. Besides, I'm not allowed to talk to strangers. I'm to go straight into school as soon as the bell rings,' she fibbed, crossing her fingers out of sight.

Her mother had dinned it into her that she was to keep herself to herself and walk straight to school. '*No nonsense along the way!*' But of course she didn't go straight in. She usually had a quick turn on the swings and the witch's hat and thought about skipping school. But she always chickened out in the end.

'Good. *Good!*' the Heron said.

The men were cautiously smiling, as if she'd passed a test she hadn't known she was going to sit.

'Now, it's very important that you don't talk to anyone about what goes on here,' the Army man said. 'The work we are conducting is of the utmost secrecy and vital to the war effort.'

He pulled some papers out of a briefcase.

'Look, I don't care what's going on here, I just want my satchel back,' she tried again.

'Never mind your satchel. Sign this. In capitals,' the Army man said, pushing a sheet of paper, yellow as cowslip, across the table.

'What is it?' She'd never signed anything in her life. 'I should read it first, shouldn't I?'

'No time! Just sign!' the Heron said, passing her a pen. 'You should have signed this well before now,' he told her, as if the fault lay with her. 'Can't believe the Commander is letting a *child* carry on living at the park.' He turned away to speak to the other two men, as if he'd forgotten she could hear him. 'If it was up to me, I'd have sent her away before now.'

'Aye, right enough! Should be adults only. Careless talk and all that,' the Army man chipped in.

The Navy man sighed. 'This is a place of work, not a playground.'

'If she'd been evacuated, as I suggested, it would have headed off yesterday's escapades at the pass,' the Heron said to the other two men, who nodded in agreement.

Why did he want to evacuate her? If Mary was being evacuated *to* Bletchley, why was this man talking about evacuating her *away* from Bletchley? She wasn't in any danger here; her father had said as much. No one was interested in a country house in the middle of nowhere. Thank goodness someone had stopped this man from sending her away. Now she had to keep her cool and not let him see that he'd rattled her.

His pen was heavier than it looked. She'd never written with a fountain pen. Mrs Ashman, their headmistress, kept one on her desk next to a pot of Velos ink, and if you'd done something worth celebrating she would write your name and then sign it at the bottom, and you could take the certificate home to show your parents. Robyn had never received a certificate but Mary already had two!

Although she didn't like to admit it, Mary was even better than Robyn was at sums. This didn't stop her from liking Mary even if her accent was different. Mary looked and sounded nothing like the other children in the class. Her father was from Jamaica and her mother from Liverpool, so her accent was a unique blend.

At first, some of the children had laughed whenever Mary opened her mouth. But once they realised she knew the answer to every one of Mr Alquin's hardest questions, they soon shut up. If only Mary was here with her now, Robyn thought. She picked up the pen, resting it snugly between her finger and her thumb, and began to read the document aloud in her best speaking-in-assembly voice.

'I'm going to read it before I sign it. "The Official Secrets Act –"' she began.

'"Is a promise which, if broken, will result in death",' the Heron cut across her.

'*Death!*' The word shot out. '*My* death?'

'Indeed. Shot by firing squad, hanging, or the maximum jail term in prison. Once you sign, you are liable to prosecution under the act for the rest of your life,' the Heron said.

Robyn stared at the three men in horror. Then realised, to her utter astonishment, that the Heron had placed a gun on the table in front of her.

5

The pen fell from her hand and bounced onto the document, splattering ink on the Heron's shirt.

'For heaven's sake!' he shouted.

Robyn had only seen a gun in real life once before. Her grandfather had one stashed in his workshop. He should have returned it when the Great War ended, and before he died he made her promise never to tell her parents that he'd let her touch it, let alone fire it. He showed her how to put matches down the muzzle, aim and shoot at the freshly painted white wall of his house. After each visit, she'd leave behind a smattering of mostly grey and brown smudges. Sometimes there'd be a triumphant red pinprick, where her match had struck home and flared.

But the squat gun on the table in front of her wasn't long and thin like her grandfather's. She'd seen plenty of big guns recently in newsreels at the cinema in town too, but this one wasn't like those either; it was much smaller. She wrenched her eyes from it. The Heron was boiling with barely concealed anger, dabbing at his ruined shirt, and Robyn was scared. The Army man pulled out another document from his briefcase and placed it in front of her. He passed her a pen.

'Sign your name.'

It was the same large and formidable document as before. How many copies did he have in there? Robyn took in the terrifying words again. She turned around in her chair. Surely the commotion over the pen – and the gun – would bring her father running into the room? But the door remained resolutely shut; maybe they'd locked it?

'Sign the Official Secrets Act.' The Heron drew out every word with irritation.

How was she suddenly supposed to be responsible for keeping everything to herself? It didn't matter because she was going to have to sign the act. And if she broke it – which could absolutely happen, even by accident, because no one was telling her what was secret and what wasn't – it would result in her death! She was only twelve. She didn't want to die!

Her hand shook as she tried to print her name in her best capital letters, taking care not to smudge them. She looked at the Heron as she passed the paper back to the Army man. She would not look at the gun. She would not!

'You have signed an oath for life and will be silent until your death. If the Official Secrets Act is broken or contravened in any way, the traitor – in this case, you – will face death by hanging or firing squad, or will be sentenced to –' the Heron began, repeating his warning.

'A traitor? Me?' she interrupted, imagining herself locked up in the Tower of London.

They had been learning about Traitors' Gate at the Tower of London with Mr Alquin for history. Wasn't one of Henry VIII's queens executed there? Or was it two? Why had women kept marrying him? She'd have run a mile. She was never getting married. She was going to be clever, like her Aunt Kate and her Aunt Eleri.

'Enough.' The Navy man passed the gun back to the Heron.

'And no more school for you, I'm afraid. You're here for the duration now,' the Army man said, taking the pen from her.

'How will I see Mary? Or keep up with my lessons? And what about . . .' She paused, seeing that it was no good and that they weren't going to budge an inch. 'If you're going to keep me here for the duration, then what will I do all day?' she asked.

They really hadn't thought this through properly, had they? At least *she* had a plan. She was going to be a mechanic and do something useful with her life. She opened her mouth to suggest her grand idea as the Heron started speaking.

'Starting tomorrow, you'll report for work duty,' he said.

'Work duty? Working where?' she asked hopefully, thinking of her father. 'In the garages?'

'In the loft. Didn't your father tell you?' the Heron said smugly. He seemed to be enjoying the fact that he knew far more about her future than she did!

Maybe if her father had been speaking to her last night, he might have filled her in on everything. But his silence was her fault for stealing the bicycle in the first place.

'What loft? Servants live in lofts, don't they? Ugh, am I going to be cleaning?'

33

'All you need to know is that you'll be helping the war effort. Your father will explain about the pigeons,' the Army man said, standing to escort her to the door.

'Pigeons? What on earth?'

Then she was on the other side of the door. And there was her father, smiling at her as if nothing at all had changed, when of course everything had.

When they got outside she stormed away from the Mansion, vowing never to enter it again. She marched across the gravel, sending stones flying, but she had to keep stopping for vans and motorcycles. So much for her dramatic exit.

'They said I'm going to be on work duty. In a loft!' she shouted when her father caught up. 'And apparently you knew all about it!' She couldn't stop herself adding, 'Why didn't you tell me?'

She'd never really felt angry with her father before. She understood, to a point, that the war had changed things, but this was ridiculous. He'd always been on her side before, especially when her mother read her the riot act, but she wasn't so sure just now.

'I wasn't best placed to speak to you last night, not with what went on and the trouble you landed yourself in. And I meant to tell you before you went in, then time ran away from me. But I can tell you now, you're to be Mr Samuels' new apprentice, in the pigeon lofts.'

'But I want to be *your* apprentice, Dad. You said you were going to teach me to drive, and I've been saving up for a . . .' She stopped, realising he wasn't even listening to her.

He kept looking back to the Mansion. He might as well move in there if he loved it that much!

'Come back inside, Birdy. I need to introduce you to Mr Samuels.'

'I'm never setting foot in that Mansion again! I'm going home and I don't want to hear another word about pigeon apprenticeships! If I can't be your apprentice, then I'm going back to school. Whoever heard of a child my age banned from going to school?' she demanded.

'Robyn! Stop!' Her father grabbed her arm. 'Please?'

'They put a gun on the table, Dad. A gun!' She shook his hand off her arm.

'Did they?' he sounded surprised. 'Did they really? Shock tactics.'

Was she going to have to spell this out to him? Didn't he realise how wrong this all was, and how frightening it had been?

'I signed it too – the Secrets Act,' her father said out of the side of his mouth.

He had one eye on her and one eye on the comings and goings by the big doors to the Mansion. She said nothing. If he thought this admission could mend things between them, he had another think coming. But she did stop stomping.

'I signed the Official Secrets Act too,' he repeated.

'Well, why ever didn't you tell me?'

'Because we're not allowed. You can't go strutting about the park shouting about secrets and signatures. Folk would guess like a shot that you knew something they didn't. And then there'd be hell to pay. You do realise how serious this is, don't you? You really can't talk about it.'

'Yes, I know! They made that *quite* clear. But I bet you weren't threatened with a gun, were you? You should have come in with me, Dad.' She tried to keep the tears out of her voice.

'But, Birdy, I tried. You saw that, didn't you? Look, are you sure about this? Perhaps you *thought* you saw a gun –'

'Of course I'm sure! I know what a gun is when it's staring me in the face. I'm thirteen, not three!'

'Not yet, you aren't. Did they tell you? You're the youngest person to sign it.' She heard the pride in his voice but was distracted.

The head gardener, Noah, and the new gardener, Kitty, were digging up the flower gardens near the yew maze, sending thorny twigs flying into the air. Robyn had never seen a female gardener until Kitty came. Didn't even know it was allowed. But then, this place was bursting with women since the war started – there'd be more women than men come Christmas. Noah and Kitty were making a lot of noise, flinging petals and soil up into the air, higgledy-piggledy. Clover, willow herb and wild poppies the colour of plum tomatoes fell on the path in front of her.

'Look, you'll soon change your mind once you see what Mr Samuels has in that loft, up in the Mansion. You'll not want to go back to Mr Alquin's arithmetic lessons and hymns in the hall then.'

'You will still teach me to drive, won't you, Dad? You won't be too busy?' she bargained.

'I promise.' He held out his hand to her like an olive branch and, as she had little choice, she took it.

6

'Here we are: Mr Samuels' office.' Her father laughed as if he'd made a joke.

When he pushed open the door, Robyn could see that he had, because there *was* no office. The long room, once filled with narrow beds where maids slept, was now an ocean of tea crates. Some were wedged underneath tiny windows, which she hadn't noticed from outside. The windows were open, letting in air, and she wrinkled her nose at the tang of the nearby brickwork factory and another musty odour, possibly damp, maybe urine.

'Ah, Robyn! Welcome!'

A heavily built man came across the room, the floorboards complaining beneath his boots. He had white curly hair and was wearing thick-rimmed glasses and khaki overalls with lots of pockets. He held out his hand for her to shake. It was crinkly, like the tracing paper at school.

'I'll leave you to it,' her father said, heading for the door.

Robyn ignored him.

'Come and meet Joy,' Mr Samuels said, his face breaking into lines and creases as he smiled.

She tried not to show her disappointment, but she really didn't want to meet another old person. She was surprised to find she wished she was at school.

As Mr Samuels knelt in front of a crate, a scuffling sound came from it.

'Is there a rat in there? Did you catch it? I could take it down to the fields and set it free for you, if you like. Or I could keep it as a pet, couldn't I?' She was already wondering where she could hide it, perhaps the plum shed. And even better, it would mean she could get out of here.

She'd call the rat George, after the king. She could train him to be friends with Lilibet and Margaret-Rose the chickens. And if she was lucky, she might get one of the chef's kittens for her birthday; she'd spotted one of the kitchen cats guarding her latest litter yesterday.

'I'd like you to meet Joy and Charity,' Mr Samuels said, grandly opening the door to the hutch.

A bird stepped from the hutch onto Mr Samuels' hand and he stood up so that she could see better.

'Why are you keeping a pigeon in a rabbit hutch?' Robyn asked, mildly disappointed about the lack of a rat.

'Look about you – there's lots of them up here, mostly squeakers –'

'Squeakers?' she interrupted. She wished he'd speak more plainly.

'Aye, young uns. Joy and Charity are my experienced carriers, along with Faith and Hope. In my humble opinion, they're the best of them. Isn't that right, my lady?' Mr Samuels cooed to the bird.

When she looked more closely, the pigeon was all the colours of the rainbow. Like a puddle of engine oil in her father's garage: glossy gold, green, daffodil-yellow, purple, pink, as well as the obvious grey and blue.

'Soft as velvet,' Mr Samuels said, more to Joy than her. As he gently stroked the bird's feathers, he spoke again. 'A bird of the air shall carry the voice and that which hath wings shall tell the matter. You might remember from your Sunday school bible lessons that Noah was the first man to realise the worth of these birds.'

'I was told to leave Sunday school,' Robyn warned him.

She really did hope that this man wasn't going to turn into one of those old people who lecture children using stories from the Bible as moral message. She'd met plenty of them before and decided they were to be avoided at all costs.

'Let me remind you, then. Noah sent a raven first, but he never came back. Happen he found a tasty treat and forgot all about poor Noah. Not the dove though – reliable as clockwork they are, have an inbuilt compass, powerful as a nail to a magnet. They use the sun by day and fly by the stars at night.'

'She is beautiful, I *suppose*. For a pigeon, that is.' She watched Joy preen her feathers.

'Aye, she is. Hand-reared her at home, just a stone's throw from here.' He nodded at the window. 'Pigeons only fly in one direction and that's home, although they can learn to have more than one home. Reliability is one of the best things about these birds. And between you and me, some of them are descended from royalty. The king's angels.'

Royal pigeons? They didn't look very royal. Tentatively Robyn raised her hand to Mr Samuels' and their fingers formed a bridge. Joy pecked at her fingers, then moved cautiously from Mr Samuels' large hand to her smaller one.

'Don't try and stroke her till she knows you. She'll soon recognise you, lass, and then you can pet her,' he advised. 'She's a clever sort, is our Joy.'

Three of Joy's pink claws pointed forward over Robyn's fingers and one long talon pointed back towards her hand. She stopped breathing and stood stock still, worried that if she moved a muscle, the bird would fly back to Mr Samuels.

'Don't fret, she won't budge. Settling, she is,' Mr Samuels reassured her as he brought out another pigeon. 'And this is Charity.'

Charity was fluffier than Joy but nowhere near as pretty, Robyn decided. Mr Samuels brought Charity close to Joy and they reached out their necks to one another.

'It looks as if they're cuddling,' she said, noting the graceful curve of Joy's neck.

'Well, they are sisters,' he said. 'Pigeons more often than not lay two eggs at a time.'

Her Aunt Kate had a daughter, Merryn, so Robyn had a cousin, but she lived in the middle of nowhere, up a mountain, somewhere in Wales. Robyn had always wanted a brother. She'd have even settled for a sister if she absolutely had to. But whenever she voiced her request, her mother said the door was closed on such matters, whatever that meant.

'. . . Princesses among pigeons.' Mr Samuels had carried on talking, looking at his birds admiringly.

'I haven't seen you at the park before, Mr Samuels. Is this a new job – looking after the pigeons?' She turned her head, taking in the hutches all around the room. There were a lot.

'Aye, I've worked for the National Pigeon Service before, but . . . well . . . not here. And as pigeon racing has been suspended now, His Maj— any road up, here we are, lass. And you're to be my apprentice with the carriers, I'm told.'

'The carriers?' It was as if he'd spent so much time with birds that he'd forgotten how to talk to people.

'"Our eyes in the skies", Mr Churchill says.' Mr Samuels smiled.

'Mr Churchill?' She couldn't believe it! '*The* Mr Churchill?'

'Oh yes!' Mr Samuels looked serious. 'Between you and me, we're doing one of the most important jobs at Bletchley.'

'What's a carrier?' Her face crinkled as she tried to understand the man's odd way of speaking.

'Carrier pigeons are driven to a destination, parachuted in behind enemy lines, then a message is attached to their capsule and they fly back home with it. Emissaries they are. I – and now you – oversee Bletchley Park's most precious cargo. See those there?' Mr Samuels pointed to a tub that was full of green rings.

'What are they?' she asked.

'Look at Joy's leg.' Mr Samuels pointed at a yellow circle with a number on it. 'It's an identification tag with a unique registration number.'

'Doesn't it hurt?'

'Not if you put it on when they're first born. Claw's nice and flexible then.'

'And it's so you can keep track of her?' she said, starting to understand.

'That's right. She can put some miles on the clock, can our Joy. And see there, that's what they carry.' He took a tiny red tube out of the capsule.

'Precious cargo?'

'That's it, lass. Quick to catch on, aren't you! They unscrew like this and round the spindle goes the rice paper with a message on.' He put Charity down next to a small water bowl, which had what looked like a slice of lemon floating in it.

'What kind of message?' she asked. Her father was right; this *was* more interesting than maths with Mr Alquin.

'Secret messages. Information we wouldn't want to fall into the wrong hands.'

'Messages about the enemy?' She gasped. Things were looking up!

Wait until she told Mary. She really ought to write and let her know why she wasn't at school. Mary'd be worried sick. Robyn never usually missed a day; her mother wouldn't let her.

'Happen you're right. It's not for us to ask. It's vital that the birds carry the right information to the right place at the right time. What we do up here is essential war work,' Mr Samuels said seriously.

'What's that bit for?' she asked, pointing to the material attached to the capsule. She wanted to know everything now.

'Protects them from chafing.' He pulled a cream-coloured

42

eggcup from a pocket on his chest, then a packet of what looked like seeds from another pocket and filled the cup.

'Is that feed?' Robyn asked.

'Yes, corn and seed. They need their fuel if they're to do the job properly. But not too much, otherwise they'll never leave this place! And they're terrible gossipers, are the girls, if they find out you're a soft touch . . . Set Joy down there with her sister, lass,' he told her.

She was reluctant to let Joy go now she knew what her top-secret job was. Joy walked forward, leading with her head as the rest of her body caught up. She'd always thought pigeons bobbed their heads, but she realised now that she hadn't been looking carefully enough.

'That water needs changing. There are more lemon slivers in the tin on the table. Helps balance their bellies. Pour the water out onto the roof.' He pointed to the open window above her head. 'And if I can tell they're not feeling tip-top, I'll pop a bit of sugar in there too. Little tonic for them, but without the gin.' He boomed with laughter.

Under the watchful gaze of Joy's wide grey eyes, Robyn picked up the water bowl and climbed onto a stool. She pushed the tiny window open, as wide as it would go. Bolshie blackbirds and colourful starlings scattered into the air. There was the familiar sound of cattle lowing and the shriek of a train as it arrived at the station across the road. She watched the water trickling down the roof tiles as a vehicle pulled up on the empty drive below. It was a hearse.

Robyn almost dropped the water bowl. The Heron's words came back to bite her – *traitor* and *death*. Someone couldn't have broken the Official Secrets Act so soon, surely? She was about to step down and ask Mr Samuels, when the Heron appeared next to the hearse. He looked around as if making sure the drive was still empty, then walked around to the big black doors at the back of the vehicle. She waited to see if a driver would get out and open the doors, but he remained in the car. What was the Heron doing sticking his beak in a hearse? He looked behind him one last time and then gingerly opened the doors. She craned her neck, desperate to see inside but at the same time terrified about what might be in there. Could it be a body? Had he? No, he wouldn't, he couldn't have shot someone, could he? She should tell Mr Samuels or Mr D! Although she had no idea exactly what she'd say, as neither of them would believe a child over an adult. The Heron lifted the edge of what looked like a heavy piece of tarpaulin and . . .

'Ready to fill her up?' Mr Samuels asked, making her jump. 'Joy is parched. So am I, as it happens. Fancy a nice cuppa, lass? I've got a brew in the other flask.'

She nodded and then turned back to the window, worried she might have missed something vital. The Heron was struggling to pull something out from underneath the tarpaulin. She waited to see what it was, leaning out as far as she could to get a better view, and was both disappointed and relieved when she saw long wooden planks instead of a corpse.

'Lass? I said, are you hungry?' Mr Samuels' voice made her start.

Reluctantly, she pulled herself back inside the loft, still clutching Joy's water bowl.

'Always,' she answered.

She hopped down off the stool and picked up the flask to fill the bowl with fresh water. Mr Samuels reached into a green bag, made of the same material as his overalls. He pulled out a brown paper parcel and the smell of pastry filled the loft.

'Evelyn – the wife – she's a corker of a baker.' He tore the pastry in half and offered one to her. 'The best baker in the whole of Bletchley, truth be told. Tuck in, lass.'

The pastry was in her mouth before she'd even thought to ask what it was. It tasted like sausage meat, peppery and rich. As they devoured their food, she gave the high window a longing glance. There'd be another opportunity to keep an eye on the Heron later. Nosing around in a hearse was extremely suspicious behaviour, although she hadn't quite put her finger on why she didn't trust him; it was just a feeling, at the moment. Even if there wasn't a dead body in the back of the vehicle, those planks were long enough to make a coffin. She wouldn't put anything past the Heron. In truth, she had absolutely no idea what he was capable of. All she had were her suspicions. And now, she was in the perfect place to spy on him.

7

'Hello,' a voice said, making her jump. 'Can I help you?'

'*Ouch!*' Robyn banged her head on the ceiling of the hearse. 'Don't you know it's rude to sneak up on people?'

'Sorry. But . . . what are you doing in there?' the boy asked.

'Nothing,' she said, rubbing her head.

'Righto. Mind out the way, then.' The boy made to shut the doors to the hearse.

She noted the lettering on the back doors of the vehicle. *Letton and Sons, Undertakers.* 'Has someone *died*?' She hesitated, not sure if she wanted the answer.

'Probably. I mean, people die all the time, but not today. If someone *does* die, we'll be back. My father says the dead pay the bills and put food on the table,' the boy finished awkwardly.

'He sounds fun,' she muttered under her breath.

They hovered around the back of the hearse, neither knowing quite what to do or say next. Robyn was wearing an old pair of Mr Samuels' overalls, sleeves folded, and trousers turned up over her boots. She was holding a smelly bucket in her hand. She'd looked out of the loft window, to make sure the Heron was nowhere to be seen, before pelting down the stairs out here.

'What's in your bucket?' the boy asked.

'Poo. Not mine. Obviously,' she added, instantly wishing she'd never said a word. 'It's fertiliser. I'm giving it to Noah, the gardener. Look – fertiliser,' she explained, lifting it up to show him.

'Righto,' he said again, moving away.

'What's your name, then?' she asked, hiding the bucket behind her back.

'Ned,' he said, holding out his hand. 'Ned Ian Letton,' he added formally. 'And you are?'

'Robyn.' She put the bucket down and took his hand, giving it a good shake. 'Robyn Audrey Lewis.'

'Pleased to meet you.' Ned withdrew his hand, wiping it on his shorts before putting it in his pocket.

It was a shame she couldn't tell this boy about the carrier pigeons. He looked the sort who would find them interesting. But she'd promised Mr Samuels, and that wasn't the only promise she'd made. There was the one on yellow paper with her name on it in capital letters. She wasn't sure if she'd ever shake that picture out of her head. She ought to stop talking to this boy and walk away before either of them got into trouble. She'd never even seen another child at the park; she had thought she was the only one.

'I'd better go, my dad will be here in a minute,' Ned said nervously. 'We have to wait until it's dark to leave,' he added mysteriously.

'Right. Well, I'd better not be late for my tea,' she replied, relieved the strange conversation was ending.

'Will you be here tomorrow?' Ned asked.

'Yes! I'm stuck here until this flaming war is over.' She shouldn't say *flaming*; there'd be trouble if her mother heard her. 'I'm here for the duration,' she repeated the awkward phrase.

'What does that mean?' he asked.

'Who knows?' She shrugged. 'They won't let me go back to school, see.' She pointed at the Mansion. 'Will *you* be here tomorrow?'

'Yes, every day until the . . . job's finished.' Ned gestured to the hearse.

'What job's that?'

This boy might come in handy as she pieced together what the Heron was up to. Sending people out to spy on children, emptying their satchels and accusing them of all sorts, was far from normal behaviour. If he wasn't careful, he'd give people good reason to accuse Bletchley Park of being a madhouse.

'Working for my father,' Ned said, avoiding her question.

'Oh, lucky you! I'm not working for *my* father, but who knows what will happen once the war is over,' she said hopefully. 'And while I wait, I'm doing an apprenticeship –' she stopped herself just in time as Ned interrupted.

'I'm an apprentice too and . . . *Oh!* I've got to go,' Ned said suddenly, looking past her. His face was a picture of panic. She expected to see the Heron returning to the hearse and got ready to run.

'I'll be by the lake, before work tomorrow morning –'

'Where's the lake?' Ned asked.

Did this boy know nothing?

'Down there.' She pointed. 'I'll show you how to make a leaf compass, so you can navigate your way about the place. Meet me down there, if you like,' she offered as a man approached the hearse at speed.

'What's a leaf compass?'

'Bring a needle. You can sneak one from your mum.'

'All right,' Ned agreed, looking nervous. 'But I'm not a huge fan of water,' he began.

'Get in!' shouted the man, who she presumed was Ned's father, 'Now, Ned. Damn it!'

'Bye, then,' she said, swinging her bucket cheerfully, despite Ned's crotchety father.

The door to the hearse slammed. The engine started up, but it wasn't loud enough to mask the man shouting at the boy, warning him to *keep his mouth shut, or else!*

8

October 1939

'Are you going to tell me any more about this new job of yours, then? We haven't had a chance for a good chat since you started,' her mother began.

Robyn hadn't even picked up a slice of toast yet, but at least her mother was speaking to her again after the trouble with the Heron and the borrowed bicycle. And her father seemed to have forgotten all about it, which was just as well, what with her driving lessons due to start today!

'It's the same every day, Mam. I feed the pigeons. I clean the hutches out and rinse the water bowls and give them their tonic,' she said, pouring a cup of tea from the pot.

'Tonic? Ha! You'll be telling me they have gin and French before lights out next!'

'Almost! I have to give them a sliver of lemon in their water if they've got an upset tummy.'

'Well, there we are, then. I've heard it all now.' Her mother tutted.

'Yes, you'd hate it,' she said, wondering if her mother could have forgotten it was Robyn's actual birthday.

'What does he want to bother with pigeons for?' Her mother shook her head.

'I don't know,' she lied, feeling uncomfortable. 'They told me I shouldn't tell,' she admitted.

She was desperate to tell her mother what Mr Samuels had said about Mr Churchill and the royal pigeons.

'Did they now?' Her mother tutted again. 'I suppose they mean well, but family doesn't count. Does it?'

'I don't know, Mam . . .' Robyn wasn't sure what the rules were, but she didn't want to risk being hauled in front of the Heron again, that was for sure.

'Never mind. I'm sure I'll be too busy working once I'm up in the big house to worry about what you're up to.' Her mother smiled.

'*What?* Why?' Robyn almost dropped her cup of tea. Were they going to make her mother sign the Official Secrets Act too?

'They've asked me to open a coffee hut, with real Lyons coffee, mind! They're already at full capacity in the dining room. All these new people, see, and more on the way!' Her mother sounded excited. 'They've even hired a pastry chef! Gave me a slice of his gooseberry pie; lovely and tart it was.'

'*You're* going to work?'

'No need to sound so surprised, Robyn. I'm quite capable

51

of holding down a job. I had a lovely job before I married your father, you know. And it will be good to earn my own money again, especially as things are going to get –'

'*You* had a job? Where?'

'I worked for your grandmother, Pat – or Mrs Lewis as I called her. We lived over the bakery with her, and she taught me everything I know. Now I'll have the chance to run my own place. It'll be more than coffee and rolls, or stewed orange tea, believe you me – otherwise your grandmother would turn in her grave!'

Robyn was dismayed. The last thing she needed right now, if she was going to get to the bottom of things with the Heron, was her mother's hawk-eyes on her.

'What on earth are you wearing? You look like a tramp!' her mother said, taking in her clothes. 'And you smell a bit!'

'It's probably pigeon droppings. Did you know that they've got saltpetre in them? They used it to make gunpowder in the olden days!' Robyn shared excitedly.

She was going to make the best of this apprenticeship. She had to prove to her father that she was the hardest of workers and deserved a place by his side in the garages.

'*Ych a fi!* Disgusting, Robyn. Not at the table, please. Why don't you get changed into something more sensible? And tidy, mind.'

'Mr Samuels gave me these overalls. They're the best thing I've ever worn in my life. All these pockets!'

'You look like a boy!' Her mother tutted.

Robyn grinned into her tea. Her mother didn't realise the intended insult was the best of compliments.

'And don't think I haven't seen those filthy boots . . . Have you been on that island again? Scullery. Now, please.'

She did as she was told, taking her boots into the scullery and setting them on last week's newspaper. Next to the paper was a small brown booklet: *What to Do in Any Wartime Emergency*. Inside was a list of Six Golden Rules, written on what her mother would call cheap-as-chips paper. She read the rules as she brushed the worst of the dirt off her boots. No. 6 was ridiculous.

'"Don't stand around staring at the sky. Curiosity killed the cat,"' she read aloud to the empty room. 'If curiosity killed the cat, the whole of Bletchley Park should be in the graveyard,' she muttered.

Some birthday this was turning out to be – cleaning boots! She couldn't believe her mother had forgotten her birthday. This would never have happened before the stupid war started. Her parents were both so distracted by it all the time. She should have been tucking into bacon and eggs and unwrapping another unexciting stack of birthday books from Aunt Kate, not eating boring old toast. She slipped *What to Do in Any Wartime Emergency* into her overalls pocket and left the scullery.

Her father was sitting at the kitchen table, warming his hands in front of the range.

'Happy birthday, Birdy. Little something here for you.' He passed her a parcel wrapped in brown paper. Then he did a double take, looking her up and down.

'You look like one of my men in the garages! About to change a tyre, are you?' He grinned.

That's the general idea, she thought as she opened the present. It was a Phillips hand-powered torch, which fit perfectly in the palm of her hand.

'Thanks, Dad!' She tucked it away in one of her pockets, delighted. 'What time shall I come down for my driving lesson? I'm sure Mr Samuels can spare me for an hour or two.'

'Eh?' Her father looked confused, draining the dregs from his tea.

'Our driving lesson,' she reminded him cautiously.

'Oh, Birdy, I'm sorry but I just haven't got time. Not today. Besides, there's so many people about now. I'm not sure it would be a good idea, not after all the trouble you've got in lately,' he said sheepishly, getting to his feet. 'Maybe when things have settled down a bit?' he added half-heartedly.

'But you promised.' She heard the whine in her voice. 'It's my birthday!'

'Now then, don't keep your father. He's got a lot on his plate,' her mother intervened, shooing him out of the door. 'We don't want both of you getting into bother with them in the big house, do we now?'

What was she on about? How could her father get into bother with the Heron? Or did she mean Mr D? Either way, her father was an adult, for goodness' sake. Adults didn't get into trouble, did they?

'Happy birthday, Birdy!' he called as he headed back out. 'I'll see you later for cake.' He winked.

He never winked at her. What was the matter with him?

He was acting oddly. She wished things would stay the same for five minutes.

'We'll have this after with candles, will we?' her mother said, placing a filled cake tin in the range to bake.

Robyn didn't think she could stomach birthday cake, she was that disappointed. She'd been waiting for this day since she first sat on her father's lap and held the steering wheel of his tractor. He'd promised her!

'Don't forget to see to the hens before you leave,' her mother reminded her as she opened the back door.

The demands of the growing numbers of staff in the dining room had forced her mother to expand the brood of hens. Robyn had considered not naming the new hens because they weren't like her pets, Lilibet and Margaret-Rose. They were the park's hens, there to feed the workers in the huts who were spilling out into the grounds of Elmer's School, which had been taken over by the War Office, just outside the park gates, and even the stable yard, which had put paid to the men testing the guns, thank goodness. Every day another gaggle of finely spoken and well-turned-out women arrived, gliding up from the railway station over the road, each carrying a small suitcase big enough to hold two changes of clothes, at best. They all went into the Mansion bright-eyed and excited but came out looking shifty and startled.

Robyn wanted to tell her mother to feed the hens herself but didn't dare. She took a few seconds to calm down, standing on the back-door step; the song of the mistle thrushes sounded like see-saws and she matched her breathing to them, her heartbeat settling back into a steadier pattern. A group of men charged past, sending thrushes bounding across the drive and up into the nearest tree. The men were wheeling big round noisy drums and carrying reams of brightly coloured wires. They were making their way to one of the barns, although she couldn't for the life of her work out how red cables were supposed to help win the war.

The hens clucked at her, impatient for their breakfast. Who knew, maybe they'd even have to get a pig, like Mr Philips whose cottage and piggery were just outside the park gates. Robyn had spent many a happy afternoon collecting the acorns for Mr Philips' pigs. *Probably can't do that now either*.

'Wait a minute! I've got something to give you before you go.' Her mother called her back in from the door, rooting around in her apron pocket for something.

'Sit back down.' She gestured to a chair.

Her mother pulled out a small box and passed it across the table. Robyn eased the lid off the box and inside sat an old penknife. It was scratched, but the initials were clear enough to read.

'W.D.? Whose initials are those?' she asked her mother, who was watching her closely.

'They're not initials, it stands for War Department. The ring is for clipping it to your belt. There's one on that shambles of an outfit you're wearing.' Her mother pointed.

'Whose was it?'

She'd been asking her father for a penknife for months. He

said she wasn't responsible enough yet. She was extremely responsible, but he was never around to see it. She'd been smugly confident that the war wouldn't take her father away from her. He was in no danger of fighting in a foreign country, because he was too old. But she'd been wrong. He was being taken away from her – just in a way she'd never expected.

'It was my father's, your grandfather – Evan-Glyn. Take good care of it, mind, because it's all I've got left of him . . .' Her mother stopped abruptly, turning around to make a start on the washing-up.

'Thanks, Mam,' Robyn said, tucking the knife into her pocket. Two presents were better than nothing, she supposed. Even if her father's broken promise still stung. She put the penknife next to the little brown book. She'd read it later in bed so that she could digest it on her own. 'I thought you'd forgotten,' she admitted.

'Don't be silly! I never forget anything important,' her mother said, sniffing. 'Happy birthday, *cariad*.'

'I'll look after it. I promise,' Robyn said, walking back over to the door. She loved it when her mother called her *cariad*. It meant something nice in Welsh, though she'd forgotten what.

'All right. Now then, haven't you got some birds to see to?' her mother asked without turning around. 'Go on, off with you. And no skulking about on that island, mind, thirteenth birthday or not!'

9

Red-beaked moorhens skimmed the surface of the lake as she waited for the mist to rise. A sleek water beetle disappeared, swallowed by something lurking in the water. Robyn pulled out her copy of *What to Do in Any Wartime Emergency*, turned to the empty page at the back and finished sketching the moorhens; she wasn't going to let the Heron stealing her sketch book stop her from drawing. She turned over a few stones with her boots, dislodging the soil, looking for an interesting piece of pottery or a fossil. She'd found plenty of treasures down here before and kept them in a Lyons coffee tin her mother had given her. She'd wait two more minutes for the boy, she decided generously, and then she'd row out to the island. Mr Samuels hadn't given her set times, unlike most of the park who seemed to be working on eight-hour shifts, even through the night. She'd watched them from her little bedroom window, filing into huts, jumping on and off buses and toing and froing from the dining room like worker bees. Even so, Mr Samuels would be expecting her to report for duty soon.

'Get in,' Robyn told the boy when he finally arrived, red-faced and panting. 'Don't worry, I'll hold it steady for you,' she added, seeing his concern as the water lapped at the boat.

'Are you sure we're allowed to use these boats?' Ned asked as he stepped in, almost capsizing it before they'd even set off.

'Sshhh. Do you want everyone to hear us?' she hissed, gesturing around to the Mansion and the huts. 'Besides, who else is going to use them?'

'Good point. And don't worry. I came from there. Hardly anyone in there this early, apart from one chap who never seems to leave. Spotted him in his pyjamas when I was working yesterday! Do you think he sleeps in there?' Ned grinned.

'I doubt it, it'd be freezing. Anyway, what were *you* doing in there?' she asked spotting a few bicycles left outside one of the huts.

She hoped to goodness one of them wasn't the Heron's, because she couldn't picture his gangly frame balancing on a bicycle. Robyn wondered what went on in the huts but remembered golden rule No. 6 from *What to Do in Any Wartime Emergency* in her pocket: Don't stand around staring at the sky. Curiosity killed the cat, and all that.

'We're building more huts,' Ned said, as she started rowing.

'Oh,' Robyn said with disappointment. Hardly exciting intel.

The boy didn't seem to be able to settle and was rocking the boat.

'I ought to tell you that I can't swim,' he admitted.

'Seriously? Why did you wait until we're halfway across the lake to tell me that?' She rested the oars for a second.

'Dunno.' Ned shrugged. 'I s'pose I'm embarrassed. Everyone in my class can swim. My dad says there's something wrong with me . . .'

'There's nothing *wrong* with not knowing how to do something. I'll teach you,' she offered, taking up the oars again. 'It's easy, once you know how.'

'Now?' Ned asked nervously. 'Can we do it another day? Because I don't think it's a good idea to start lessons now because I didn't bring my bathers with me and –'

'No! Not now, don't be daft. It's October! Swimming doesn't start until May and is well over by September,' she explained.

She rowed efficiently, steering them around the back of the island, away from any huts. When they reached the island, she tied the boat to the trunk of her favourite willow tree. Robyn offered the boy her hand. The last thing she needed was him falling in and making a splash.

'So, what do we do now, then?' He sat down on the ground, crossing his legs. He had his grey school shorts on, and his skin was goosepimpling in the early morning breeze.

'Did you bring a needle?'

'Couldn't get one. Dad caught me going through Mum's sewing box and there was what for . . .' He clammed up.

'S'all right. We'll do the leaf compass another time. I'll get you a needle, no bother. And a magnet,' she promised, sensing Ned's discomfort.

Her mother would have been delighted if she'd caught Robyn rifling through her sewing box, but the last thing she'd use a needle for was sewing: they had much better uses. But if he didn't have a needle, a penknife or a magnet, then what *was* he keeping in his pockets?

She changed the subject. 'I come out here to watch the birds and draw them. If you like, I'll show you my best climbing tree, that's where I spy on the Mansion from.'

'Why are you spying?' Ned asked curiously. 'You shouldn't be spying, should you?'

'I'm not *technically* spying if I live here. I've got more right than most. I'm just keeping an eye on comings and goings. Only watching what *certain* people are up to from my own back door. I mean, be honest, haven't you noticed anything strange about this place?' she asked casually. 'All this "need to know" nonsense. How are we supposed to know what we need to know in advance? It's completely impractical.'

'My dad says I don't need to know anything other than to do as I'm told,' Ned said.

'Well, it turns out, Ned, that fathers don't always know best.'

He closed the topic by rummaging through his pockets before pulling out an empty nutshell.

'What's that?' she said, giving up on cracking any secrets Ned might be keeping from her for the moment.

'A nut whistle.'

'Where'd you get it?' So, the boy *did* have something of use in his pockets.

'Made it.'

'How?'

'S'easy. You take an almond, biggest one you can find, and sand it down.'

'What if you haven't got sandpaper?' she asked, turning a clay stone over to see the animals underneath it. 'Hello, mister woodlouse!' She held out her finger.

'You could try rubbing it against a rough wall until you make this end flat and then a hole should appear. You have to make another on the side. There, see?' He showed her.

'That's clever,' she said, admiring his handiwork.

'And Bob's your uncle!' He took it back, put it to his lips and blew quietly.

'It's not as good as a tin whistle,' she said.

She'd ask her mother for an almond later. The brick wall of the outhouse would be perfect for sanding it.

'Come on, time to go,' she announced. There were pigeons to tend to and Herons that needed watching. 'You don't want to be late for work, do you?' She hoped this leading question might . . . well, lead somewhere, but Ned simply nodded.

They stopped by a snaggletoothed bramble thicket that was dropping polished plum-coloured blackberries. She grabbed a few and handed some to Ned. They were late this year.

She wanted to ask him if he'd had to sign the Official Secrets Act. Or if they'd waved a gun in his face. But the memory of the Heron in the Mansion stopped her in her tracks.

Robyn could see the other rowing boats now. They were neatly lined up by the wooden landing stage. Who they were waiting for she had no idea. Someone had added another eight boats to the set, freshly painted too. Presumably for some adult to use, although she couldn't think who would have the time or the inclination to go boating on the lake – *don't they know there's a war on!*

Thanks to Ned and his father, and a small band of groundsmen, more wooden huts were being assembled by the lake. The park was starting to look like a building site.

'Are you off up there?' Ned gestured to the loft, after they'd tied up the boat.

'Yes. Are you back down there?' She pointed at the huts as they crossed the lawn – sending starlings, who'd been scouting for worms, up into the air – and reached the main entrance to the Mansion.

'Yes,' he said noncommittally.

She wondered how long it would take her to find out precisely what Ned's father had told him to shut his mouth about. A gulp of glossy swallows swept over their heads, their beaks full of finds and their long tails streaming out behind them. They'd be leaving soon, taking their chatter and rattle with them. The stable yards, where the swallows liked to roost, were now a cacophony of constant noise. They might decide never to return, what with all the disruption going on at the park. And really, she couldn't blame them. It was as if the war was forcing everything to run to a different time and order, even the animals and the plants.

'Will I see you later?' Ned asked hopefully.

'Course. By the lake. I'm usually down here if I'm not in the Mansion.'

'All right,' Ned agreed reluctantly, 'but can't we meet somewhere else? Like by the sundial?'

She felt sorry for Ned. He was missing out, stuck building huts with his crosspatch of a father. Of course he couldn't *know* what he was missing in the lofts, having never been up there.

Just at that moment a dispatch rider, with crisscrossed leather satchels and a dark armband, stopped their motorcycle right in front of Robyn and Ned. They pushed their goggles up onto their forehead.

'Do you know where a . . . Mr Knox is?' the rider, a girl, asked them, double checking the name against a small notebook.

Before either of them could answer, a tall shadow fell, cast by a figure hurrying out of the Mansion at pace.

'I'll take whatever you have for Mr Knox. Thank you, Sadie.' The Heron held out his long-gloved hand.

'Sir.' She nodded. This Sadie seemed to know the Heron.

She rifled through her satchel and then handed over a stack of brown files. The Heron signed something quickly while Ned took that as his cue to leave and ran off towards a partially constructed hut.

Robyn stood motionless, waiting to see if the Heron would recognise her or, worse still, want to speak to her. She wished she could turn into one of the gothic stone griffins either side of the Mansion entrance, right beside her. As the courier drove off, the Heron spun around to face Robyn, leant in close and reached out his gloved hand without saying a word.

Is he going to hit me? His hand was inches from her face.

Then he removed a rolled-up cigarette that some joker had stuck in the mouth of one of the griffins and pulled away from her. He growled then threw it to the ground in disgust. It was as if she was invisible to him. He stamped on the cigarette and ground it aggressively into the gravel with his foot. Seizing the moment, she turned and ran past him into the Mansion. She took the stairs two at a time, desperate to reach the sanctuary of the loft, Joy and Mr Samuels' easy presence.

10

A pigeon shuffled around on a wooden board by one of the entrances to the loft. The board banged as the pigeon moved, causing a bell to ring.

'That's a clever mechanism,' Robyn said, examining the device.

'Aye,' Mr Samuels agreed, lifting his head from one of the hutches.

'How did you make it?' she asked, keen to have a go herself, if he'd let her. Finding out how things worked in here might be useful to her later once she was working in the garages.

'I attach the board to a circuit, and it sets off the bell trap, over there.' He pointed to where the bell was. 'Lets me know when one of the birds comes home.'

Mr Samuels carefully removed a green capsule, with a splodge of white on the end of it, from a pigeon's leg.

'Is there a secret message inside?' She was unable to hide her excitement.

'Aye, lass,' he said.

'Are you going to open it now, Mr Samuels? The paper must be tiny and so thin inside. You'll need a magnifying glass to read it, won't you?' She cast about, looking for one in the room, wanting to be helpful. 'I could find one for you, if you wanted. Or even read it to you, if you like?'

But Mr Samuels didn't open the capsule. Instead, he picked up a telephone receiver. She hadn't noticed the telephone yesterday. It was black. Red would have been more exciting, even though she was sure they did the same job.

'Head of Operations: Special Section, NPS. Dispatch rider needed at once. *Codename: Dov* . . .' Mr Samuels said quietly.

The last word sounded like *doves*, but Robyn couldn't be sure. Didn't he mean pigeons, not doves?

'I can answer the telephone for you. I'm ever so polite. I could jot down any messages,' she said as he replaced the receiver.

She was keen to see what these messages might be about because so far, despite signing the secret document, not that many secrets had been shared with her, which was a great disappointment.

'And my handwriting is improving, Mr Alquin says,' she added to sweeten her suggestion.

She had to make herself useful. If Mr Samuels offered a good report to her father, he might finally take her on in the garages. It wasn't as if he had many boys to choose from now. Most of them were desperate to go to the war, and she needed to get in there before they all came back and tried to take her place.

'I'm sure your penmanship is grand but you're not to answer the telephone under any circumstances. *Certain people* don't think children should even be here at the park –'

'But I'm not a child,' she interrupted, thinking of Ned. 'I'm thirteen now. Anyway, why shouldn't children be at the park?'

'Some folk think that children shouldn't be in a place like this,' Mr Samuels said. 'That they'll not understand the need to keep quiet.'

'But that's ridiculous! I've signed the Official Secrets Act. I'm excellent at keeping my mouth shut. Honestly, you wouldn't believe the kind of things that I've got up to . . .' She stopped before she gave away too much.

'Well, as it happens, I don't necessarily agree with them, lass, but what can I do?' He held his hands up in the air. 'A word to the wise: keep your head down and stay out of them downstairs' way.'

'All right,' she agreed. He sounded just like her mother.

'Good. Now then, pass me that logbook.' Mr Samuels pointed to a plain notebook next to the clock.

Taking a small stub of pencil from behind his ear, he wrote in the notebook. He crossed something out and then wrote two more things down. She'd have to start keeping a pencil behind her own ear. It could be useful for her drawings. When Mr Samuels put the logbook away inside one of his many pockets, she wished she could open each one to see what was in there. Then she'd copy him and fill her own pockets with the same things.

'Well done, lady, well done.' He stroked the bird's head

with his thumb then carried her to one of the hutches, away from the window and light.

'You deserve this, Faith,' he told her, taking the eggcup and brown paper bag from his pockets.

She watched, noting how much feed Mr Samuels gave the carrier pigeon.

'Would you see to Joy, lass? She's got an eventful time ahead of her,' Mr Samuels said. While he focused his attention on the returned pigeon, who looked exhausted, Robyn was glad of the chance to do something useful. She noticed a large wicker basket sat on top of Joy's hutch.

'Is Joy going somewhere?'

'She is that. Depending on weather conditions.'

'Weather conditions?'

Robyn used the excuse of looking out of the window at the weather to check if the Heron was still skulking about by the entrance to the Mansion, but all was clear.

'I didn't fancy that mist and mizzle earlier – they can lose their homing instinct if the fog's thick.'

'Maybe I should go outside and keep an eye on the weather?' she suggested hopefully. She wanted to know where the Heron had snuck off to with Mr Knox's files that he'd intercepted from Sadie, the dispatch rider, earlier.

'You could take that capsule down when the courier arrives. First, there's work to be done, and then we'll stop for a breather and a brew and see what Mrs Samuels has put in the pack-up.'

She nodded happily. Waiting for the dispatch rider would give her the perfect excuse to ask a few careful questions and cast about for the Heron. And she wouldn't mind finding out how a person became a dispatch rider in the first place, if there was time to chat.

She opened Joy's hutch and moved back to let her out. Joy was beautiful, she thought, watching the light changing the colours on the pigeon's chest. Admiring her pointed wings, Robyn imagined Joy's muscular body sleeking through the sky and reached into her pocket to pull out her notebook in the hope of capturing some of Joy's impressive physique when she noticed something was wrong.

'Mr Samuels! Her feathers are falling out. Are they supposed to do that? Is there something wrong with her?' she shouted in alarm. 'Come and look, please!' She held three feathers up to show him.

'Let's have a little deek at her.' He stepped across the room, weaving his way in and out of boxes, tea crates and hutches.

'Not to fret, she's moulting, that's all. She'll be looking hailsome again once her new coat comes in. Might make up some formula for her with a splash of Pearson's.'

'What's in the formula?' she asked, wondering what Pearson's was.

'Good strong Yorkshire tea, toast and my secret ingredient. They're the long-distance runners of the bird world. We need to treat them like athletes.'

'What can I do for her?' Robyn asked, looking at Joy. 'Water and feed, I know, but is there anything she needs wherever she's going?' She was dropping hints, desperate for Mr Samuels to let her in on Joy's secret mission.

'Water, food and your company.' He ran his hands over Joy's body. 'Hmm, this might change things.' He seemed to be thinking aloud, looking around the room at the other hutches.

'Won't it make it easier to fly if she's lighter?'

'Nay, lass. She needs her new feathers to come through. These old ones are like me – worn out, they are.' Mr Samuels smiled as he explained.

'Does it hurt her?'

'Well, now, there's a question. No one's asked that before.'

She couldn't help but feel pleased. Her father loved her asking questions, or at least he used to, when he still had the time to answer them.

'They scratch more than usual when the new feathers are coming in. Makes them tired.'

'We could move her to one of the quieter corners?' Robyn suggested. 'I could look after her, couldn't I? I wouldn't mind sleeping next to her hutch, in case she needs me.'

'Mebbe.' He nodded. 'Although I'm not sure what your father would have to say about that!'

'He wouldn't even notice, he's barely at home any more,' she said, earning a thoughtful look from Mr Samuels. Maybe she ought not to have said that.

'Where was Joy supposed to be going? Behind enemy lines, was it, Mr Samuels?' She'd heard the glamorous phrase spoken by several women in the Mansion and been desperate to try it out herself.

He nodded. She gasped: he'd finally let her in and confided something more than details about daily routines. *Now* things were getting interesting! He might even confide the secret ingredient in Joy's special formula.

'But if Joy is going to be flying in the face of danger, she might never come back. What if she gets injured somehow and can't find her way home?' she asked in panic.

'Joy's been training since she was a squab. She knows her way home. It's deep in her soul.' He patted his chest. 'For a pigeon, home is where the heart is.'

'Well, I don't think Joy should go if she's shedding. I mean, moulting.'

'That's as may be, lass. We'll see,' he said.

Mr Samuels prised the lid off a tin. He passed Robyn a square squashed-fly biscuit. 'Not quite birthday cake. She wanted to make you a teacake, but the birds don't like the smell of cinnamon, so squashed fly will have to do. Many happy returns, lass,' he said.

Her father must have told Mr Samuels it was her birthday; she shouldn't be quite so hard on him. The biscuit was mouth-wateringly delicious. He was right, Evelyn-the-wife was a wonderful baker. Though not as good as her mother, of course.

Robyn waited for the dispatch rider to collect the capsule while broad-chested buzzards circled above, their mewing calls echoing as they plummeted from the sky in wide arcs. She searched inside the mouths of the two stone griffins, but disappointingly they were now free of cigarettes. Was everyone terrified of the Heron? They ought to be more concerned about what Mr D thought of them. If they were at school, the Heron would be more like Mr Alquin: not the top of the food chain, like Mrs Ashman, the head, but still important and able to rule the roost a bit. The significant difference between the men was that Mr Alquin, her teacher, was strict but kind, while there didn't seem to be an ounce of kindness in the Heron.

Robyn waited for the dispatch rider to collect the capsule, wondering if it would be the same woman as earlier – Sadie, the Heron had called her. She might have come back to collect whatever response Mr Knox had. That was assuming the Heron had ever actually delivered the files. The dispatch rider Mr Samuels had called might be a different one too. There were so many of them turning up at the park these days: she'd counted thirty last week. They arrived, delivered or collected a message and then sped off with it, to wherever it needed to go next. A lot of what went on with the capsules and motorcycles was a mystery to Robyn. Still, she'd think of the right question to ask the rider. She wasn't a schoolchild any more. She was an apprentice to . . . What was it he'd called himself on the telephone? Head of Operations of Special Section? Wait till she told Ned! But then Robyn remembered she couldn't tell Ned anything. *Or could she?*

11

'Mary? What are *you* doing here?' Robyn was shocked and delighted to see her best friend heading towards the great doors to the Mansion.

Could it be they'd realised how horrible and mean they'd been to ban her from school and had let Mary come to the park just on this one special occasion? You didn't turn thirteen every day.

'Robyn!' Mary said, breaking into a huge smile. 'Happy birthday!'

'Thank you! Oh, wait a minute. I've got to um . . . speak to this err . . . rider,' she stammered. How was she to explain to Mary why she was waiting for a dispatch rider?

The capsule felt the size of a train carriage in her pocket. Turning away from her friend, she covertly pulled it out, hid it in her hand and ran over to the dispatch rider. It was Sadie.

'Here it is,' Robyn whispered to her, and she looked puzzled. 'It's from Mr Samuels: Head of . . . the Pigeons.'

She'd completely forgotten Mr Samuels' title in her shock at seeing Mary. *Head of the Pigeons* sounded absolutely ridiculous.

The dispatch rider took the capsule. She placed it carefully in her satchel and swung it over her head before starting up the engine of her motorcycle. *There goes my chance to ask questions.*

'Robyn, what are you doing up and about? I thought you were ill,' Mary said, walking over to her.

'Up and about?'

'Everyone at school said you had chickenpox. That or diphtheria. Or measles. Owen James said you'd gone to live in the madhouse. He tried to take over Bird and Tree club, charging us double, so I gave him a dead arm!'

'Owen James is a menace. He told me a spot of nonsense about you too. Well done, he's had that dead arm coming a while now.' Robyn grinned. She had missed Mary so much. Ned Letton was all right, but not a patch on her.

Robyn thought about all the questions she'd planned to ask the dispatch rider. Well, there'd be time for them tomorrow or even sooner. And she'd managed to deliver the capsule without any mishap.

She looked Mary up and down. 'Where did you get that bag?'

A new satchel, like the dispatch rider's, was strung across Mary's chest and she was wearing a peaked cap.

'Isn't it super? I'm to keep all the letters and mail for people on the park and other bits of paper in it but I'm not to look at them, or open them, obviously! I've never had a new bag.' Mary smiled. 'Always made do with Sybil's cast-offs and hand-me-downs.'

'Very fancy. You look like a postie. And what is that on your head? Hang on, what *are* you doing here? Did my mother invite you for birthday tea?'

"Fraid not. No time for tea and cake, I'm working.' Mary beamed at her.

'What?'

'I'm one of the messenger girls,' Mary said. 'And believe me, there are a lot of messages being passed here, from dawn till dusk! Not that I'm allowed to work that late.'

'You're working *here*? At the park?' Robyn asked in disbelief.

'Ta-dah!' Mary twirled.

'Is that why you're wearing trousers instead of your school skirt? You never wear trousers.'

'Neither do you!' Mary replied. 'What's that get-up? You look like you're off to join the forces!'

Robyn looked down at her own overalls and laughed.

'Who'd have thought it?' Mary said looking around. 'Me, in a fancy place like this! It's like something from a fairy tale. There's even turrets!' She pointed to the Mansion.

'But why aren't you in school?'

'Mr Alquin said he'd taught me everything he could. Said he had something more suitable in mind for me, more challenging. Told me he had an old friend who was looking to take on an apprentice.'

'What?' Robyn pulled Mary by the hand, away from the Mansion.

They ran over the little bridge and down into the walled garden, where they'd be able to talk out of sight.

'Start at the beginning and tell me everything!' Robyn demanded.

'After he marked my last arithmetic paper, Mr Alquin showed it to his friend, over a pint. He said his friend was always on the lookout for bright young things. That's what he called me – *a bright young thing*! Can you believe it?' Mary said.

'I can! It's the perfect description of you, Mary.'

'I went to Mr Alquin's friend's cottage for an interview. And you'll never guess who came through the back door!'

'Who?' Robyn could barely keep up.

'Your mother! With some cakes. I'm surprised she didn't mention it.'

'You were in Mr Knox's cottage?' Robyn checked. '*My* next-door neighbour is Mr Alquin's friend? And my mother was there?'

'Yes! Anyway, I had to sign a piece of paper with all kinds of promises on it and look, ta-dah! I'm a Bletchley Park messenger girl,' Mary held up her bag, which was exactly like a postmistress' satchel.

It flipped open, revealing several large thick envelopes poking out. There were names and numbers on them. She quickly looked away, not wanting to compromise her best friend.

'Where are you living now, then?' Robyn asked. She wondered if her mother would consider letting Mary stay with them. They could top and tail in her bed – like sisters!

'Same old,' Mary sighed.

'You didn't escape the dreaded Mrs Fisher?'

'No! I'm stuck lodging with her until I can find a better place to billet. I'll be lucky, though. From what I hear, every spare room in town has been taken. There's talk about billeting women in Woburn Abbey! Can you imagine? La-di-dah! Not that I'd want to be that far away from you. If only I'd been evacuated to your mother. Her *bara brith* cake was delicious. One of the ladies gave me a wedge of it while I signed some papers.'

'Mam said she wasn't allowed to take in any evacuees. I begged and begged her. I didn't really understand why not, but now it makes sense. I thought Mrs Fisher was going to send you back to the school board and make you stay with someone else?'

'She ate her words when Mr Knox sent one of his ladies around. She told Mrs Fisher how much she'd get for my keep, now I'm working,' Mary said. 'Mrs Fisher said such mean things about her afterwards. Women shouldn't wear men's clothes, and that her bow tie meant she might be one of *those ladies*.' Mary looked puzzled.

'Don't listen to a word she says. Mrs Fisher is a bad sort altogether. I love wearing my overalls. And look at you in your fine trousers. We both look very smart,' Robyn said forcefully, wishing she could give Mrs Fisher a dead arm. 'I'd rather be one of *those ladies* than Mrs Fisher any day! She looks like she runs on pure rage.'

'It gets worse. Once the lady had gone, Mrs Fisher called me a fly-by-night. She grabbed my ration book as soon as I set foot in the door,' Mary sighed. 'Even so, I bet she'll still serve up mashed potato on toast.' She screwed her face up.

'What about your parents and Sybil?'

She knew how badly Mary had been missing her family back in Liverpool. Mary had expected her big sister, Sybil, to be evacuated with her, to Buckinghamshire. Instead, she'd stayed with their mother and father in the city. Robyn pictured Mary hopping on and off trams, buses, trains and ferries. Dashing about the city, meeting people from different countries and speaking different languages. This worldly sophistication was why Mary was allowed to roam free about the park, while Robyn was confined to the pigeon loft, which smelt of bird wee.

'Won't your family worry about where you are and what you're doing?'

'I've written to them and told them I've found a job,' Mary said smiling.

'You didn't tell them what you're doing, did you? Or where?' Robyn asked in alarm, remembering the Heron and the prison sentence or worse he had scared her with.

'No, I said it was for a local business. They told us to reassure our families that we're well and enjoying the experience. I try to do that. Mam was cross at first that I'd left school, but Dad's that proud of me.'

'Oh, that's good. That's great!' Robyn said in relief.

'So you don't have chickenpox? Then why've you been off school all this time? Mr Alquin wouldn't tell us anything, no matter how much I begged him,' Mary said.

'I'm an apprentice in the pigeon loft –' she began.

'What? Why?' Mary interrupted.

'First, they made me come in here to the Mansion and then they interviewed me and . . .' She paused. She really didn't want to spoil things by talking about what had happened in that room with the Heron. There was no need to frighten Mary.

'Interviewed by who?' Mary looked confused.

'Never mind all that. We're both working now, so no more lessons!'

'No more schoolbooks!' Mary added.

'And absolutely no more teachers telling us what to do and when!'

Mary smiled. 'We can see each other whenever we like now! And I've got so much to tell you. A lot has happened.' She grinned. 'I've missed you!'

'Oh yes! Me too. And it's going to be so much fun having you here. I've got to go, but meet me by the lake before and after work? It can be our special spot.' She smiled back at her best friend. 'Oh, and if you get a tea break, bike down there then too.'

'I've got an even better idea!' Mary's eyes lit up. 'We could leave notes for each other in the griffins' mouths!'

'No! Not there, it's too dangerous,' Robyn shook her head, thinking of the Heron. 'How about in the library? Between the pages of a book?'

'Oh, clever idea. What'll they have in there? Hmm, definitely Shakespeare. There's bound to be a copy of *Hamlet*,' Mary said confidently.

'I've never read it. What's it about?' she asked.

'Deception and death.'

'Ugh. Who'd want to read about that?'

'Exactly! No one will take that out. It's always *Romeo and Juliet* or *Macbeth* or *Henry V*.

'All right,' Robyn agreed, '*Hamlet* it is.'

It was impossible not to be swept up in the excitement. Although the war was showing no signs of slowing down, with Mary by her side, everything was infinitely brighter.

12

Robyn was surprised to see Mr Samuels wasn't wearing his usual overalls when she arrived in the loft. Instead he wore a heavy double-breasted woollen coat and a pair of dark trousers. His soft white curls were flattened down with liberal amounts of Brylcreem. And his glasses were sparkling and clean, not a smear in sight.

'Where are you going?' she asked.

'Off to Windsor to deliver the birds . . .' He paused.

'Not Joy?'

'Not Joy,' he confirmed. 'Keep watch for me. Note down any arrivals in the logbook. I've set down a bag of feed over there.'

'But when will you be back?'

'Before dusk.'

'Don't you need someone to go with you?' she asked hopefully.

'Aye. Your father's coming along,' Mr Samuels said.

'*My father?* Why?' she burst out. 'What's he got to do with the pigeons? Shouldn't he be in the garages?'

It didn't seem fair that her father was allowed to go where he pleased, and when, but she wasn't.

'He's driving us,' Mr Samuels explained.

Her father arrived to help carry four travel baskets, with pigeons inside, down the stairs. 'It'll take more than one pair of hands to load them up and drop them off for release,' he said, as if this should explain everything.

'Release?' Robyn asked. 'If I'm going to be an apprentice up here, instead of with you, then shouldn't I come with you and Mr Samuels? I'm supposed to be learning how it all works, aren't I?'

'Now, Robyn, we've already talked about this,' her father began.

'I could help you, Mr Samuels, if you need more hands . . .' she offered, ignoring her father. 'I'd be no bother. You'd barely even notice me.'

Her father gave her a final look of warning.

'Now, lass, you're not to fret. I'll be back to help you feed the rest of the pigeons at dusk,' Mr Samuels repeated.

'But –' Robyn began.

'Watch Joy for me. Keep her away from the windows,' Mr Samuels cut her off.

'All right,' she agreed reluctantly.

'And remember what I've taught you and you'll not run into any bother or strife.'

Bother and Strife were her middle names, Robyn thought, watching the two men leave, taking the pigeons with them. Once again, she found herself on her own. But then she remembered Mary! And Ned too, she supposed. Being on her own in the loft for the day might not be so bad. She could invite Mary to come up there. She'd leave a message for her in *Hamlet*. If her father and Mr Samuels were going to abandon her and keep her in the dark, then she might as well have some fun. It shouldn't be too hard to whisk Mary through the Mansion. The Heron was always in his study with Miss Hughes, or out of the way skulking around the park. Even better, he might be off site too. Off site seemed to be a choice available to everyone but her.

She slipped down to the library, first checking the Heron's door was shut and the coast was clear, and left a quick note for Mary inside a copy of *Hamlet*, then seized the opportunity to run outside and grab some fresh air. It really did stink in the loft! When she bumped into Ned getting some tools from the hearse she felt duty bound to invite him up to the loft too. Although she worried that Mary might find him a bit dull.

'Are you sure we're allowed up here?' Ned asked, following her up the stairs, eyeing the door to the loft.

'Stop worrying,' she told him, dodging the question.

'Isn't it against the law or something?' He waved his arm around vaguely.

'Everything's against the law now we're at war, Ned. Hadn't you noticed?'

'Robyn knows best. She has lived here all her life, after all!' Mary said.

'Exactly!' she agreed. 'And I'll be stuck here for the rest of my life too,' she added, sighing dramatically.

'Wait a minute . . . Is it, though? I don't want to get the sack. I'm getting on nicely with Mr Knox,' Mary said smiling.

'Who is Mr Knox?' Ned asked.

'Look, I haven't been *explicitly* told not to bring you up here, put it that way.' Robyn shrugged.

'That's not an answer.' Ned stood firm, arms folded.

'And there's plenty of other stuff I have been told in no uncertain terms not to do,' Robyn continued.

'That's not very reassuring. And who is Mr Knox?' Ned repeated.

'Mary's boss. Besides, Mr Samuels won't be back until dusk and no one else ever comes up here.'

'I've only got a quick break,' Mary reminded her, dropping Mr Samuels' messages on the top of an old bureau.

Robyn watched as Mary moved some seed packets aside, laying the files out neatly. She had to find out if those files the Heron took from Sadie had reached Mr Knox. Mary could investigate on her behalf.

'I think we should scarper,' Ned said, checking the door again.

'Stop worrying. Robyn's an apprentice, after all,' Mary reminded him.

'So am I,' Ned said flatly, pulling a face. 'I'm going to be an apprentice undertaker.'

'Yes, *yes*, we're all apprentices!' said Robyn. 'Now, Mary, you feed that row. Ned, the middle, and I'll take the back row. All right?'

She watched Mary and Ned scoop eggcups of grain out of the sack Mr Samuels had left. Ned knocked over a bowl of feed. It clattered across the wooden floorboards. Unlike Mary, she very much hoped Ned *would not* stay all day.

He was as jumpy as a jack. They didn't need anyone from downstairs coming up to see who was making more of a racket than a watch of nightingales. The Heron's door, near the library, had been shut when she checked, but who knew how long he'd be in there for.

'Sorry! Eggcup's a bit slippery is all. What you need is one of those scoops,' Ned suggested, as if he knew better.

'Never mind scoops, hurry up. We need to get a move on,' she told him.

'To be honest, Dad won't miss me while he's in the huts with the numbers men. I'd rather not be stuck in there – it's so stuffy, the huts are blue with smoke. He's setting them up with some coke stoves – have you seen the way those flames blow up into the air? Getting ready for the big freeze they say is coming.'

'I suppose I'd better let you in on my plan, Ned. Three heads are better than one and all that,' Robyn said generously, hoping her trust in Ned wouldn't be a mistake.

'Yes!' Mary agreed. What's this all about, then? Is it about *this place*?'

'Yes. I mean, it's all very well dragging us out of school and giving us jobs, then putting the frighteners on us and forcing us to sign the Official Secrets Act – with guns on tables,' she began, but Ned and Mary's expressions stopped her.

'*Guns?*' Mary looked horrified and turned to Ned.

'Who has a gun?' Ned leapt up and ran to the door to check if anyone was coming, as if he were expecting an armed ambush at any moment.

'Didn't they put a gun on the table when they questioned you?' She faltered.

Was her father right? Could she have imagined it?

'Who questioned you?' Mary put a hand on her arm.

'Umm . . .' She was speechless.

'I had a chat with Mr Knox in his kitchen, and he said I couldn't tell anyone what happens at the park or I'd go to prison. Obviously I'm *not* going to tell anyone. So, I signed the . . .' Mary paused and then whispered, '*Official Secrets Act.*'

'You didn't even go into the Mansion?' Robyn checked.

Mary shook her head. Robyn made a mental note to demand her satchel back. She hadn't even told Mary about her book yet. She'd have to replace it if the Heron decided to keep it. But if he didn't give her back her earnings from the Bird and Tree club, how was she going to do that? He was the most impossible and unreasonable man! Might Miss Hughes have a soft side? Mary could butter her up with some of her mother's scones; it was certainly worth a try.

'What about you, Ned?'

'My father took me into the sentry hut by the big front gates, you know, where the guards are stationed. They told me I had to keep my mouth shut, or else. My father's always telling me to keep my mouth shut, so nothing new there.'

'And that was it?' Robyn checked. 'None of the guards had guns? Not even a small one?'

'If they did, I didn't see any.' Ned shook his head. 'The man warned me not to mention the name of this place to family or friends.'

'All right. Enough. Tell us what happened to you,' Mary insisted.

Robyn took a deep breath and told them what had happened with the Heron in that dreadful room.

'I can't believe they'd do that to you!' Mary looked disgusted.

'They can't go through your things like that, can they?' Ned asked.

'If he won't give you my book back, then never mind,' said Mary. 'I've already joined the Bletchley Park library. There's more in books in there than I've ever seen in my life, and I'm going to work my way through them. He won't stop me reading, don't you worry! Mr Knox says the ladies have a secret collection of their own in all kinds of different languages!' Mary finished.

'Thanks, Mary, you're the best. I still can't believe it happened, but then I see him about the place and remember how horrid he was. Especially when he saw our secret language. You should have seen the way he looked at Miss Hughes. It was like *I* scared him for a second, instead of the other way around –'

'What do you mean, *your* secret language?' Ned interrupted.

'You know, like ones you make at school, with your best friend.' Robyn waved her hand at Mary. Surely Ned had codes and languages with his own friends?

'Are you going to use it now? Here?' Ned looked both jealous and worried.

'Course not! It's for babies, isn't it?' Mary laughed.

'Erm, no! It's not for babies.' Robyn was hurt and annoyed. Why was Mary pretending it didn't matter? Was it because of Ned? 'It took you ages to work it out, Mary. Why would you say that?'

'Obviously we won't be using it. It was silly, really.'

'Just tell me!' Ned said impatiently.

'All right. It's a two-wheel code. The alphabet goes on the first wheel and doesn't move, then you turn the second wheel, which also has the alphabet on it. That's the code. It's extremely basic.' Mary shrugged off Ned's curiosity. 'My dad showed me how to make one.'

'Well, I thought it was clever!' said Robyn. 'And we described everyone around us as an animal, so we could talk about them in code and no one who heard us would understand what we were on about – that was my idea, Ned. We renamed places, so school was the prison and BP was the madhouse. Mr Alquin was the owl, because of his spectacles and how he knows everything. And Mrs Ashman, our headmistress, was the lioness because she was queen of the jungle.'

'And Owen James was a dung beetle and horrid Mrs Fisher was a hyena. But, like I said, it's silly. We won't be using the Caesar cipher again,' Mary insisted.

'I'm going to rip it out of my sketch book, once I get it back. I might even burn it too,' Robyn threatened. That'd show Mary who was silly.

'If you're sure,' said Ned. 'Because if you are going to use it, then it makes sense that I learn how too. Because . . . well, because they might be suspicious of us now. Robyn lives here all the time, so they might be worried about what she might see or hear, because –' Ned began hesitantly.

'Ned Letton! Stop *becausing* the life out of things! And are you suggesting I might blab? Or let something slip?' Robyn said indignantly. 'And don't you dare defend the Heron!'

'Of course, he wasn't defending the . . . *Heron*, is it?' Mary intervened. 'Don't you know his real name? And aren't you basically using our secret language by calling him that? And why did you draw our wheel in your sketch book?'

'In case I lost the one you made me. Besides, I wasn't thinking about our secret language, *actually*,' she lied. 'It just came to me. He's gangly and spindly and stalks everywhere like he's looking for prey. You'll see what I mean when you spot him. Strutting about the place as if he's always lived here! I'm the one who was born here, not that outsider. And if anyone should be acting like the king or queen of Bletchley Park, it really ought to be me, not some strange interloper wheedling his way into our business and stealing my things!' She curled her lip. Thinking about the Heron set her teeth on edge.

'Well, whatever this big secret is, if it's important enough to scare children by searching them and taking away their bags and books and, even worse, threatening them with guns, like we're the enemy, then they shouldn't wonder we want to find out about it!' Mary declared supportively. 'They're acting like they're in some kind of murder mystery novel!'

'Yeah! And forcing us into the world of work.' Ned shuddered. 'I've seen enough dead bodies to last a lifetime! It's only fair that they give up some of their secrets in return!' He punched the air.

Robyn had underestimated him. He might not be such a mouse, after all. 'Well, I'm not going to stand for it. If they won't give up the secrets willingly, then I'll –' She was on her feet, getting into the swing of her speech.

'*We'll!* We're a team,' Mary jumped up to join her. '*We'll* find ways of taking them. By force, if needed!' she shouted.

'Steady on. Not by *force*!' Ned said, also getting to his feet. 'My friend Kevin says there's a madhouse at Bletchley Park and I don't want to end up in there!'

'Don't be daft, Ned, there's no madhouse here . . . Is there, Robyn?' Mary scoffed but looked to her friend for confirmation as the telephone started ringing.

They all looked at one another and stopped talking. It rang several times before stopping abruptly. Robyn sighed with relief and carried on the conversation.

'Of course not. You'd do better not to listen to silly boys like Kevin,' she told Ned.

He sounded a lot like Owen James.

'Kevin's dad is in the RAF, so he thinks he knows everything. We never hear the end of it. Adrian who lives next door, his uncle's a naval officer, and he agrees with Kevin about the madhouse and so does Gary. That's all I'm saying.' Ned held his hands up. 'This place is like a rabbit warren: rooms and huts and shed and turrets and domes. They could be hiding people anywhere in here and you might never know. I've heard there's a secret –'

The telephone rang again, and the birds started shuffling, as if they'd had enough of the sound too. This time Ned and Mary nodded at Robyn, as if she should answer it. They waited until it stopped, and Robyn sighed in annoyance and tried to remember what she'd been about to say. She'd never answered the telephone before, Mr Samuels hadn't trained her, and he'd specifically told her not to answer the telephone. Besides, she didn't want to embarrass herself in front of Mary and Ned. What if she got it all wrong?

'There's no one hidden in the park, Ned. Don't be ridiculous. This is my home – don't you think I'd know? Now, first thing we need to find out is what my boss is up to off site.' She liked the way *boss* sounded. It made her feel ever so grown up. 'Off site,' she repeated longingly.

'Is he meeting someone who needs carrier pigeons to take a message to one of the Allies?' Ned suggested.

'Oh yes, well done, Ned! He didn't tell me who he was meeting, but I heard him say *doves* on the phone. *I think*.'

She needed to pay more attention to Mr Samuels. She'd start by tucking a pencil behind her ear to make notes with. Then spend less time drawing Joy and more time writing down his telephone conversations.

'Doves? Thought they were all pigeons.' Ned looked around the loft in case he had missed some.

'Doves and pigeons are the same, aren't they?' Mary said.

'That's like saying you and Sybil are the same, just because you've got the same parents. Or Ned and his brothers.' Again Robyn silently cursed her parents for forgetting to give her a sibling.

'Sorry, sorry.' Mary held her hands up.

'Doves are plain and small, and pigeons are all the colours of the rainbow and big. Anyway, I've heard Mr Samuels say *doves* before, or at least I think I did. It could be code,' she said with more confidence than she felt.

'Code for what, though?' Mary shut the last hutch.

'I don't know, do I? That's the whole reason the two of us are teaming up, isn't it?'

'The *three* of us, right?' Ned checked, looking momentarily crestfallen.

'Sorry, Ned, I didn't mean to forget you. I'm a bit nervous about overseeing the loft. It feels like I've swallowed a colony of butterflies.'

The phone rang, making them all jump and reverberating through the floorboards.

'Shall I answer it?' Mary offered. 'It must be important, if they keep ringing?'

'No! If anyone's going to answer it, it'll be me,' Robyn said with authority.

She jumped up and ran across to Mr Samuels' desk. It didn't seem like the telephone would ever stop ringing. Although Robyn was sure it wasn't possible, it felt like the noise was getting louder and louder. It was bothering the birds.

'What should we do?' whispered Ned. 'Someone might come! I told you we shouldn't be in here.'

'Why are we whispering?' Mary asked, giggling nervously.

'Stop it!' said Robyn. 'This is not a laughing matter. This is serious business. Vital war work! Mr Samuels gets important calls from especially important people and writes things down in his notebook. But he's not here so I'm going to take the call and write the message down.'

And before she could think better of it, she picked up the telephone and said, 'Hello?'

'I'm his main messenger girl,' Mary continued proudly. 'He asked for me, specifically.'

13

'It's not as if she's going through Mr Samuels' diary or wallet!' Mary said encouragingly.

'And I doubt it'll turn anything up,' Robyn said in agreement. 'I need to find out where they've gone.' She ignored Ned, sifting through papers and little drawers.

'Adults say all kinds of things for *reasons* that don't make much sense,' Mary added. 'We've all got parents, haven't we?' She laughed.

Admittedly, it felt awkward sneaking around the loft while Mr Samuels was out. He might be on a vitally important and top-secret operation, but after what Robyn had heard on the telephone, they had little choice but to act.

'Tell me what they said again,' Mary prompted.

'All right. I said "Hello" and then the voice said "Special Section, NPS?" I said "Yes" then they said "Codename?" and I said "Doves". Then the voice said, "Rendezvous cancelled" and I said "All right" and then they hung up.'

'How did you know what to say or how to answer? I'd

have been completely lost.' Ned sounded admiring.

'I've heard Mr Samuels on the phone plenty of times and I tried to say the same things,' she said casually, although she was quite impressed with herself.

'Rendezvous is French for meeting,' Mary said. 'Do you think it's wherever Mr Samuels and your father are going?'

'It could be?' Robyn shrugged. 'This is the trouble when adults start acting all cloak-and-dagger. How am I supposed to help them if they keep me in the dark?'

'If you're right, how will we let them know it's cancelled?' Ned wondered.

'We don't! *We can't!* I wasn't supposed to pick up the phone, was I, because I'm not supposed to be up here. Mr Samuels told me children are not wanted at the park. How are we going to warn them?'

What if Ned was right and her father and Mr Samuels were in danger? Arriving with carrier pigeons for a cancelled meeting could place them both in harm's way. She'd never forgive herself if anything happened to her father. She hadn't even said sorry for all the trouble she'd got into with the Heron. Or for sulking over the lack of driving lessons.

'There's no point in panicking. Your father and Mr Samuels can take care of themselves. They'll show up and see no one is there and head back here,' Mary offered.

'You're right. They might even be going to a completely different meeting,' Robyn said.

'Anyway, didn't you say you had something to show us?' Ned tried to change the subject.

'Oh yes!' She led them over to Joy's crate, opened it and

held her hand out for the pigeon to step onto. 'This . . . is Joy.'

'Is she special or something, then?' Mary looked unimpressed. 'They're all over the city centre at home. Liver birds, we call them. You know I'm from Liverpool, and we've got these really tall buildings with birds that watch over us. Legend says if they fly away, it'd be the end of Liverpool. Anyway, one of them did a dropping on my mam's hat once. She said it was good luck but Sybil says they're dirty, like rats with –'

'Don't say it!' Robyn interrupted. Even though she may have said it herself, once or twice, she never wanted to hear the comparison again. 'They're actually very clean birds, always grooming each other.'

'Sorry!' Mary said.

'I can't believe you can't tell the difference between Joy and some plain old city pigeons! There are hundreds of different breeds, Mary!' Robyn might have expected Ned to react this way to Joy, but never her.

'Carrier pigeon, isn't she?' Ned checked. 'Not a common wood pigeon?'

'*Yes, Ned!* But she's moulting now. Confined to barracks,' Robyn said, remembering the phrase Mr Samuels had used. 'Needs some rest and recuperation, Mr Samuels says,' she said pointedly to Mary.

'I can see why she's your favourite. There's something special about her, isn't there?' Ned said.

She was glad at least one of her friends understood what she saw in Joy.

'How do you tell them apart?' Mary asked, peering into one of the many hutches. 'They all look identical to me.'

Perhaps Mary should get back to her rounds and messages. 'By the markings and colours on their feathers. And their movements and mannerisms.' She paused for thought, trying to remember everything Mr Samuels had imparted. 'And Joy recognises me now,' she said confidently.

'I bet it's more that she knows she's on to a good thing and you'll feed her,' Ned teased.

'She probably recognises your smell,' Mary suggested.

'Aren't you the charmer?' Robyn was still smarting from the comment her mother had made about how she smelt. She'd have to make sure she scrubbed down in the scullery a bit more regularly.

'I wasn't saying that you stink! The pigeon recognises the smell of your skin, like dogs do,' Mary tried to explain.

'I don't think that's how it works.' Robyn shook her head.

It was a good job Mary was so clever. She clearly didn't have a future as a naturalist. How could anyone compare a pigeon to a plain old dog?

'Anyway, like I said, this is Joy and she's Mr Samuels' speediest flyer,' Robyn continued. 'She's supposed to be going on a . . . Well, anyway, she's grounded until she's finished moulting –'

'What on earth is going on here?'

The three of them jumped up from Joy's crate. Startled, the pigeon flew up into the air before settling on one of the beams.

'I asked you a question!' the Heron said, standing as still as a statue. 'Did I hear a telephone ringing?'

What was *he* doing in the loft?

'We're . . .' Robyn struggled for an answer, looking to Mary and Ned for help.

'Looking after the pigeons?' Ned offered.

'And I was delivering a message to Mr Samuels,' Mary said, pointing at the post on the bureau.

'Who are *you*?' the Heron demanded, looking down at Mary. 'What kind of message?'

'I work here,' Mary began to reply, but the Heron didn't seem interested in hearing her answer. 'It's in the envelope on his desk. I don't know what kind of message, sir.'

'Looking at you, I doubt that very much that someone like you works here,' the Heron accused. 'You're a foreigner.' He pointed a long, gloved finger at Mary again.

'I'm not a foreigner. I'm from Liverpool,' Mary replied proudly.

'Hmm. That's as may be. Did you open it? Did you read it?'

'Of course not!' Mary tilted her chin at him. 'I'm one of the messenger girls and we *never* open any of the messages. Mr Knox trusts me, sir.'

'Does he indeed? Curiouser and curiouser,' the Heron said sarcastically.

Robyn moved closer to Mary and at the same time so did Ned. They stood united, facing the Heron.

'She does work for Mr Knox. I should know – he lives next door to me,' she backed Mary up.

'Goodness, you are a little know-it-all, aren't you?' He shook his head at Robyn, before turning his attention back to Mary. 'And I suggest, if you are who you say you are – and, believe you me, I will be checking – that you get back to work, miss. Now, do as you're told and pass that message to me, thank you very much. That's it, quick smart!' The Heron held out his hand for the message, then turned to speak to Robyn again, 'I understand Mr Samuels is still off station, correct?'

'Yes,' she replied.

How did he know everything? *Off station, off site.*

'As for you, lad, what are you doing up here with the Lewis girl?' The Heron turned on Ned. 'Shouldn't you be helping your father?'

The Lewis girl?

'I'm Mr Samuels' apprentice!' She couldn't stop herself from blurting angrily. 'Not *the Lewis girl*!'

'I know exactly who you are, *miss*. I've got the full measure of you and what you're up to. Answering telephone calls that have absolutely nothing to do with you – I said you couldn't be trusted, and most certainly not *up here*.'

'I *can* be trusted.'

'Silence! I've had just about enough of you already. Your father and Mr Samuels will be hearing from me. You, miss and you, undertaker's boy, out!' The Heron held the door open for Ned and Mary.

'Children consorting! Whatever next?' he muttered to himself. 'No place here whatsoever! And now there's three of them listening in on telephone calls and reading notes. Multiplying like rats!' He sniffed the air with disgust before holding a crisp white handkerchief over his nose.

There was no point in arguing with an adult, so Mary and Ned left the room. Robyn was sure they'd find one another later. The woods might be a better meeting point than the loft; she'd leave a note in *Hamlet*, if she could get to the library later. Robyn waited until the Heron had marched out after her friends, then encouraged Joy back down and into her hutch, slamming the door shut.

'Good riddance to bad rubbish!' she said to Joy.

She hadn't even heard the Heron walking up the stairs; it was as if he'd appeared from thin air. And she'd made sure he was in his office before she found Mary and Ned. Why was he sneaking about? What if he *had* he heard her answering the phone and what she'd said? She'd be in so much trouble with Mr Samuels and her father when she'd promised to be reliable and look after things in the loft.

Did the Heron know what *Codename: Doves* meant? Perhaps he'd sent her father and Mr Samuels off site on a wild goose chase, leaving him free to creep into the loft and look for more files and messages to steal, because he most definitely didn't care about the pigeons. Robyn wished she'd opened the message Mary delivered before the Heron took it away. How was Mr Samuels going to know what was in it now? And didn't that make both Mr Samuels and Mr Knox victims of the Heron's thieving, which in turn surely made the Heron . . . a spy! But if he was a spy, how were Robyn and her friends going to prove it?

The clock in the tower chimed noon as she got her breath back and her temper in check. She had a few hours before Mr Samuels and her father returned. But would there be enough time for her to speak to them before the Heron did?

14

Gritty grains of soil snuck under Robyn's fingernails. She was rooting around for more bugs and snails for the pigeons. Mr Samuels said they helped the birds' digestion as they were full of vital fats. She had no trouble finding ants and earthworms around the damp base of an ash tree; and scooped some into one of her mother's jam jars. As she entered the woods, hoping to find some words, she spotted Mary and Ned.

'What are you two doing in here?' she asked.

Ned laughed. 'Cycling lessons. I bumped into Mary, or rather she bumped into me!'

'Have you seen him? I've looked everywhere but he's completely disappeared,' Robyn said, exasperated.

'He's not down by the huts,' Ned said, immediately guessing she was talking about the Heron.

'I've been all over the park but didn't spot him.' Mary shook her head, trying to keep balance on her bicycle. It was the small dark-green one the guard had accused Robyn of stealing. It didn't seem fair that she wasn't allowed to use it but Mary was.

'Ned's *trying* to teach me how to ride.' Mary pointed at a cut on her knee. 'We thought it best to lay low for a bit with the Heron on the warpath.'

'Might as well have some fun before I get frogmarched out of here and home for a telling-off . . .' Ned faltered, his smile nowhere near convincing enough. Robyn knew a thing or two about how that felt.

'Mr Knox says I'm to learn where every office and department on the park is, but he won't give me a map – too dangerous,' Mary said.

'I can draw you a map on the ground,' Robyn offered, looking around for the right stick. 'Although it'll be out of date in a few days, the rate this place is changing!' she joked, thinking about the Anderson shelters she'd seen being assembled earlier by Ned's dad and a few other men, down by the tennis courts. She hadn't seen Ned with him, which was strange.

'Hold on there!' Ned grabbed Mary, who was about to topple off her bike.

'Watch you don't get a puncture! There's hawthorn in here,' Robyn warned. 'And mind your lights when it gets dark, otherwise you'll get a ten-shilling fine from WPC Lawrence.'

'Oh yes! My father gave me a talking-to about looking after my tyres yesterday. There's not enough rubber to go around,' Ned warned.

'Let's teach her together!' Robyn suggested to Ned. 'I

know how to balance with a basket on the front and I bet you don't, Ned Letton.' She winked at him.

'Untrue! Baskets aren't just for girls. I've got one on my bicycle and very handy it is for putting things in. All right, let's find a flatter path,' Ned said.

Keeping her hand on Mary's back they negotiated the tight twists and turns of the damp forest floor. The ground was littered with hazel and ash leaves, and in one place the dead brittle branch of a fallen elm.

'I need a hot drink,' Ned declared blowing on his hands. 'And something to eat.'

'Oh yes, d'you reckon your mother would give us a bun from her new coffee hut?' Mary asked as she hopped off the bicycle. 'I'd kill for a hot chocolate.'

'Don't be daft! I'm not going anywhere near my mother! Or her coffee hut.' She shivered in the shade. 'I bet the Heron's swooped down on her already and filled her in on my latest escapades. It'll be early bed and no pudding for me tonight. Or worse.' She sighed and tried to ignore the unpleasant flutters in her stomach. It wasn't that she set out to get into trouble; it just seemed to find her.

'But I'll keel over if I don't eat something,' Ned said.

He took the bicycle from Mary, wheeling it back to the edge of the woods.

'All right, *all right*. I'll see what I can rustle up,' Robyn offered, following him. 'But I'm not promising high tea at the Ritz.'

'I'll deliver some of these messages on the way,' said Mary. 'This large one is for Mr Knox. I could slip round there, couldn't I?' She held up one of the bigger envelopes from her satchel as she jogged to catch Ned up.

'Hang on, where did you get that message? Was it delivered by a dispatch rider?' Robyn asked hopefully.

'Yes. Why?' Mary asked.

'Because a dispatch rider came with a message for Mr Knox earlier, but the Heron flew off with it. I bet he never gave it to Mr Knox, and I wondered . . .' She tailed off.

'We are not opening Mr Knox's messages. Not a chance!' Mary said vehemently, tucking the envelope back in her satchel.

'We could steam it open over the kettle. I've done it before when school sent a report home,' she confessed. 'Mr Alquin had some mean things to say about me, which I didn't feel were true.'

'Robyn! Do you want us to get into serious trouble, even more than we are already?' Ned said, shocked by her admission.

'Oh, come on, Ned. There's a war on, don't you know? People are meant to take risks! Couldn't we take a quick peek? No one would know.'

'Absolutely not!' Ned shook his head.

'Speaking of peeking, I have to tell you, Ned, I think your father might be mixed up with the Heron.'

'No!' Ned steered the bicycle out of the trees and back onto the park. 'Sorry, Robyn, but you've got the wrong end of the stick. My dad's the straightest man you'll ever meet.'

'Well, I saw *him* – the Heron – with his head in the back of your father's hearse. Your father didn't get out, he just let the Heron root about in the back, completely unsupervised. The Heron was pulling the planks about and measuring them. And do you know where your father was this morning?' She folded her arms across her chest, presenting the case to Ned.

'No. Why?'

'He was here. Without you. Building Anderson shelters by Hut 4. Hefting sandbags about and setting up a stirrup pump, in case of fire.'

'Oh. Well, that sounds harmless enough, maybe he was . . .' Ned struggled for an explanation.

'But why didn't he bring you with him?' Robyn demanded.

'I don't know, he just told me to cycle in later.'

'Hmm, that's a bit suspect, isn't it? Anything to do with the Heron means he's up to no good,' she said with confidence.

Mary grasped the situation. 'You think Mr Knox's stolen files and Mr Samuels' message and Ned's dad's hearse are all linked, somehow?'

'It's too dangerous,' Ned said.

'But what if he *is* a spy?' Robyn reasoned.

'My father! Impossible.' Ned laughed. 'I'm telling you, he's the most patriotic person I know. Plays by *all* the rules. An absolute stickler for them.'

'Not your father, you ninny. The Heron. What if he's stealing information and he's going to hide it in a coffin?' Robyn threw her hands up in the air.

'But why would he hide it in a coffin?' Mary asked.

'I don't know! He's odd, isn't he? And oddballs behave in odd ways, don't they?'

'But that doesn't make him a spy, Robyn! Look about

you! This place is full of odd people,' Ned said gesturing to the lawn. 'They can't all be spies.'

A rounders match was taking place, with a commentary given in what sounded like Latin. Men in jackets and ties stood shivering, shouting and clapping every now and then. The umpire appeared to be Mr D himself, though she hadn't seen him in person for years, just glimpses through the Mansion windows. He was blowing a whistle and laughing, commenting on the action in a broad Scottish accent. Quite different to the man she'd heard stories about around her kitchen table. Just who were all these people? There must be almost a hundred or so, some in forces uniform and others in civilian dress.

'All right, they're an unusual crowd, I'll give you that, but they're not all sneaking about or stealing messages, are they? Look at them – they're running around chasing a ball, just like we used to do at school. But the Heron isn't here, is he? He's not like the rest of them. And if he finds something out and gives it to the enemy, it could put your brothers in danger. And everyone here at Bletchley.'

Ned said nothing, but she could tell she'd made him think.

'All I'm saying is, let's keep an eye out, the three of us. Mary, you can watch Mr Knox and the cottage and look out for the Heron turning up. Try not to let him take anything,' she suggested.

'How am I supposed to stop him?' Mary's eyes widened. 'Have you seen the size of him?'

'I don't know, you're a *bright young thing*, aren't you? Work it out. Ned, you can find out if your father knows the Heron, and why he was so interested in your hearse –'

'It's not *my* hearse! I can't stand the stupid thing,' Ned interrupted. 'Just sitting in it gives me the shivers.'

'All right, all right, we get it, you don't like it, and I'll admit it's creepy, but do your best. And I'll get to the bottom of *Codename: Doves*. And make sure the Heron doesn't get the chance to go through Mr Samuels' records,' Robyn suggested.

'Look, I can't question my father, he wouldn't like it. I'm to be *seen and not heard*. But I can keep an eye on the Heron and the hearse. If he comes down to the huts we're building, I'll find out what is going on,' Ned offered, and she could tell it had cost him a lot.

'Deal.' She held out her hand and he shook it.

She offered her hand to Mary, who did the same. They would have smiled, but this was serious business.

'I've got a chart tacked up on my bedroom wall, now I've *finally* got it to myself,' Ned said, changing the subject. 'I'm following the progress of the Allied advance across Europe. The BBC daily bulletin tells me exactly what the movements are and then I mark them out. White pins for the Germans and black for the Allies. Red and blue for my brothers, although I'm not sure where either of them is right now.'

'Very clever, Ned!' Robyn said.

'Rob and Joe, they're my brothers, they taught me all about the enemy planes. You can get these picture guides in the newspapers with silhouettes of plane –'

'I have those!' Robyn interrupted, thinking about the paper aeroplanes hanging from her ceiling like ghosts. Her father had a Public Warning aeroplane-spotting poster tacked up in the garages, which she'd studied, but she didn't want to steal Ned's glory.

'And I can recognise them by sight and some by ear,' Ned said.

'Your observational skills will come in handy, once I've worked out a strategy to deal with the Heron,' Robyn said, impressed.

'Once *we've* worked out out!*!*' Mary reminded. 'We keep telling you, you're not on your own any more.'

'Sorry! So, what do you think they do in the huts all day, Ned? I tried to look through the windows, but they were all taped up and covered with blackout curtains. I know we're not to ask questions but it's only natural to wonder why they made us sign that paperwork . . .'

'Stop, Robyn! Not another word or . . .' Mary held her hand up.

'Or what, Mary? They'll do away with us for daring to ask?' She was fed up with all this secrecy even though she understood the reasons behind it. 'But really, anyone would be hard-pressed to get information out of us. We know less about the goings-on here than the enemy does!'

'*Shush!* You never know who's listening,' Mary said, looking over her shoulder. 'There's eyes and ears everywhere.'

'If we're going to come up with a plan, then let's do it inside, away from beady-eyed Herons and walls with ears,' Ned suggested.

'There's no walls out here, dafty,' Robyn replied, but he was right.

'There's walled gardens and a maze – mazes have walls, don't they?' Ned countered.

'Come on, then, clever clogs, this way to the *war council meeting*!' she stage-whispered, taking the bicycle from Ned. 'I'll be Chamberlain and you can be –'

'How come you get to be the prime minister?' Ned argued.

'Because it's my kitchen and my idea,' Robyn argued back, as they kept to the shadows, and out of the adults' sight. 'But we'll have to keep our voices down. Mr Knox and the ladies are busy working on particularly important things . . .'

'That's right,' Mary said. 'They're always running about the place talking in tongues and shouting "Eureka!" when they work something out. What it is, I don't know, but they get extremely excited about it. And one of them wears trousers and bow ties. *Looking sharp*, my dad would say.'

Mary liked to talk about her dad – a lot – and the things he would say. Although it was interesting, especially as Mary did her dad's Jamaican accent, *sometimes* Robyn wished Mary would stop going on about him and how great he was at Morse code and singing and telling jokes.

'Yes, yes, clever clogs. You'd fit right in with Mr Knox and his ladies. Anyway, as I was saying, they're just next door and even though the walls are as thick as Owen James' –'

'Can we please stop talking about walls!' Mary interrupted, making them all laugh.

15

'I'll take this in to Mr Knox.' Mary pulled out the large envelope and made her way to his front door. 'Back in a flash.'

Ned followed Robyn down the red-brick passageway which separated her cottage from next door. They heard Mary knock and enter the cottage. They waited, looked at each other, then waited some more. After a little while, Ned gestured to the clock tower, which they could see from the passageway.

'She's taking her time, isn't she?' Ned finally broke the silence as the clock chimed. 'What if the Heron has already been to see Mr Knox and is going to give Mary her marching orders? If they send her home, she could be bombed. She's from Liverpool, isn't she? We'll never see her again.' Ned sounded desolate.

'Pull yourself together, Ned, you've only known her five minutes! She's *my* best friend. Look, let's sneak around the back and look through the window.'

Robyn reached out her hand and pulled him across the grass behind her cottage. When they reached Mr Knox's leaded window, she dragged some milk crates underneath it and gestured to Ned to climb up with her. She hopped up, put her fingertips on the windowsill for balance, and peered in.

Mr Knox was sitting at his desk, wearing his horn-rimmed glasses and stuffing his pipe. Robyn took in the four young women who always surrounded him. *Dilly's Fillies*. She didn't like it; women weren't horses, that name was just silly. She'd been in and out of the cottage running errands for her mother and delivering cakes, so the ladies were all quite familiar to her now. Three of them dressed in plain shirts, cardigans and skirts but one woman, the tallest, and her favourite, wore a pair of high-waisted, wide-leg trousers and a bow tie. All three were talking at once, peering over Mr Knox's shoulder. Reams of papers streamed across the desk and pooled onto the floor at his feet. The tall woman with the bow tie leant forward and snatched up a piece of paper. She circled words with a red pencil triumphantly then handed it to one of the other women, who typed something into an ancient-looking typewriter with flashing lights.

'Looks like it's from a museum,' she whispered to Ned.

'An antique,' Ned said wisely.

'Wonder why they don't have something modern to work on, like the women in the Mansion,' Robyn thought aloud.

'Never mind that, where's Mary?' Ned asked. 'Where did she go?'

'I'm right here.' Mary tapped Ned on the shoulder, making him gasp.

111

'Sshhh! Mary.'

Robyn looked past Mary, expecting an adult to come running and tell them off again. Instead, the sound of jazz music started up, followed by laughter and voices. She couldn't stop herself from creeping back up to the window.

'Shove over.' Mary climbed up onto the milk crate to see.

Mr Knox was stood in front of a gramophone conducting and the ladies were all dancing, as if in celebration.

'Aren't they smashin'?' Mary said admiringly.

'Aren't they supposed to be working?' Ned whispered back.

'They are working. They're puzzling the messages out. See that typewriter thingy. When they press a letter, another pops up in lights, but it's a completely different letter. They've got to work out what the code is, I think,' Mary suggested.

'Oh, that's what they're doing! I thought they had an old machine. The ones in the Mansion are so much better, all shiny and new.' Sometimes Robyn wished she knew as much as Mary.

'That still doesn't explain the music and the dancing,' Ned protested.

'It's Duke Ellington, Dad's favourite.' Mary bobbed to the beat. 'Dad works at the shipyard now, but he was in the Navy, in the Great War. He sold his saxophone to buy his passage to England. He was worried he'd miss out on the war; he wanted to do his bit,' Mary added.

'Didn't your father want to go home after the war was over?' Robyn, thinking that the war didn't sound that *Great*.

'No. Not once he got used to the cold. He'd met Mam

when he was singing in a music hall. My Nana Rene took him in. Dad says he arrived in Liverpool like a string bean and Nana turned him into a broad bean.'

'I'd hate to be in the Navy. Can't stand water.' Ned shuddered, then admitted to Mary, 'I can't swim.'

'Oh, Ned. I'll teach you if you like. I'm going to join the WRNS when I'm old enough. They're the Women's Royal Naval Service. Once you're a Navy family, you're always a Navy family, Dad says.'

'Aye, aye, captain!' Robyn joked, saluting Mary. 'That would suit you, working for the WRNS. And wrens are highly intelligent and friendly birds. Oh, and they're excellent singers too!'

'How do you know all this?' Ned asked, his stomach rumbling.

'My dad. He's full of stories, especially about birds. Apparently, if you harm a wren, it's said it'll bring you bad luck, like a broken leg or something.' Robyn shrugged. She didn't believe everything her father told her.

Ned's stomach rumbled again. 'Tell us what happened in there, then?' he prompted.

'I knocked on the door and the women pounced on me and took the package. They opened it and spread it out on Mr Knox's desk and then started speaking in another language,' Mary explained.

'What language?' Ned asked, intrigued. 'German?'

'Italian, I think.' Mary hazarded a guess.

'How do *you* know Italian?' Robyn queried, trying not to sound jealous.

'Mr Alquin gave me lessons after school. We did some Latin too,' Mary explained. 'And Morse code, although I already knew that, thanks to Dad.'

'Ah! So that's what Owen and Thomas were on about – your special lessons. How come you never told me about them?' Maybe Mary really *was* going to go to university.

'You never asked.'

'Come on, then, Ned. Let's sort your belly out.' Robyn gave him a little push then ran along the path which led back round to her cottage.

'What's that under your arm?' she asked Mary as she held open the back door.

'*Alice's Adventures in Wonderland*,' Mary said, putting the book down on Robyn's kitchen table.

'Never heard of it,' Ned said, pulling up a chair in anticipation of something to eat.

'It's a story by Lewis Carroll. He's Mr Knox's favourite writer. In fact, they're friends!' Mary said, as Robyn grabbed some scones from the pantry and put them down on the table. 'It's got brilliant illustrations – you'll love all the animals, Robyn. Shall I read it to you?' Mary opened the colourful pages and spread it out on the table.

'Ugh, no,' Ned said, taking an enormous bite out of his scone.

'Go on, then,' Robyn replied at the same time.

She poured her mother's elderflower cordial into glasses as Mary told them the story of Alice, and the strange new world in which she found herself.

16

Robyn waited by the side gates next to the Mansion, on the lookout for more dispatch riders, as well as the Heron. Had he and Miss Hughes shown her papers and money to anyone? Or was he keeping her belongings out of pure spite? She peered through the iron bars, hoping to spot Mr Samuels and her father returning from whatever covert mission they'd been on. When the clock tower chimed three, Robyn returned to the loft to clean out the cages. At four o'clock she poured a cup of water into a bowl for Joy and the other birds, adding a pinch of sugar from the pot Mr Samuels kept next to the telephone. Her fingers itched to pick up the receiver and listen. She willed the telephone to ring as she stirred the sugar in the cup, waiting for it to dissolve, then placed the bowl in Joy's hutch.

By five o'clock, there was no sign of Mr Samuels or her father and not a single phone call. It was teatime; her father never missed teatime. It was the one meal they always ate together as a family, no matter what. She imagined Mrs Samuels in her cottage, sitting by a clothes horse in front of the range. Robyn pictured a pot of tea warming and a cake or pastry cooling. Mrs Samuels – Evelyn-the-best-of-bakers – must be wondering where her husband was. Robyn reached into the hutch and felt for the top of Joy's head. She was asleep, so she seized the moment and stroked the pigeon's thinly covered skull. It felt oily, like St John's wort, which grew down by the lake.

'Why isn't he home yet?' she asked Joy, as the pigeon slept on, growing her new feathers. 'He said he'd be back by dusk. You know him better than me, Joy, but I feel like Mr Samuels is the kind of person who wouldn't lie or break a promise; he's always talking about Mrs Samuels and making sure he's back in time for her baking. He's a good sort, I think. Is he a good sort, Joy? I mean, you've spent more time with him than I have. You'd tell me if he was bad news, wouldn't you? He's nothing like the Heron, that's for certain. I wouldn't trust *him* as far as I could shove him into the lake.'

Robyn removed her hand, not wanting to unsettle the bird.

'I'm willing to bet that Mr Samuels has never left you in the lurch before, has he, lady? Talks to you like you're the princess of the pigeons,' she chattered on.

'Something isn't right,' she decided at last. 'He'd be back here if he could, which means he can't get back and something bad has happened to him. And my dad. And only I know about it. Maybe I should tell Mr D, if I could get to his study without the Heron spotting me. But would he listen to me? Would he take *me* seriously, Joy? No, you're right, he wouldn't, but I know someone he would have to listen to – my mother! Thanks, Joy! You've been a great help.'

Robyn scattered a handful of sunflower seeds from her pocket and closed the hutch. As she ran down the stairs, it felt as if everyone in the Mansion lifted their head, paused for a moment, caught her eye, and then looked away, uninterested. They were used to her running about the place now.

'Ah, the Lewis girl,' a familiar voice boomed. 'Stay right there,' the Heron continued, swooping in on her from who knew where. 'I want a word with you.'

She hated him calling her *the Lewis girl*. His rumbling voice made her feel like a rat in a trap. She closed her eyes and wished she could will him away, package him up like a parcel and send him off with a dispatch rider, somewhere far away from her and Bletchley Park. Why couldn't he go and poke his blasted beak into someone else's business, instead of always interfering in hers? If she didn't know better, she'd swear he instinctively knew where she was, as if he were a hunter and she his prey. She tried to pluck up some courage. Her mind filled with images of his gun, his brown-leather-clad finger on the trigger. *Traitor. Death.*

'Come with me. This way,' he said, spinning on his heel with the confidence of a man used to being obeyed.

The Heron walked with his head tucked in close to his shoulders and his gloved hands clenched behind his back. Why did he always wear gloves indoors? What was he hiding?

Robyn followed him back through the hallway, past the ballroom. The clattering of teleprinters and telephones bounced off the oak-panelled walls inside. A few weeks ago, the room had been empty.

Robyn tried to make eye contact with one of the nice-looking women typing away in there. The woman was concentrating on the big brass keys. Robyn desperately wanted someone to see what was happening, and where he was taking her, *just in case*.

She followed his sombre dark grey jacket and trousers which barely reached his dark grey shoes, his thin legs were that long. He marched past the library, a small room, filled with leather-bound books with golden writing on the spines. There was no one in there, but a cream cardigan with a blue trim hung off the back of a chair next to a small brown leather handbag. It would take an eternity to read all those books, Robyn thought, but Mary would be up for the challenge.

'Keep up, do!' the Heron cronked.

He stepped into his study, with its perfect view of the lake. She pictured him perched motionless on his chair, watching her on the water. What if he'd seen her with Ned and Mary? She wasn't really scared for herself, as she was often in hot water, but she didn't want to land her friends in any trouble. It sounded like Ned had enough of that at home.

The Heron shut the door. Robyn could still hear the piercing ring of telephones and the low thrum of voices. She wished he had left it wide open because she didn't want to be alone in a room with him, especially without Miss Hughes being there. Robyn should have run past him and found her mother, just as she'd planned to do before he reared his ugly head.

'Sit,' he said, pointing at a chair in front of his desk.

Robyn would have preferred to stand, but she obeyed.

The Heron stalked around the desk before folding himself into his own chair. He impatiently swatted away a fly. The room smelt overpoweringly of floor wax and tobacco. There was a wire tray labelled IN and another labelled OUT. Both were overflowing. Robyn stared at the paintings framing either side of the desk, rather than meeting his eye.

'Ah, yes, I forgot, you like to think yourself an artist. All those scribblings and drawings. You have a connoisseur's eye for art?' he said with unveiled sarcasm, getting up suddenly to stand in front of one of the paintings, taking his glasses off to clean them on a crisp handkerchief. 'It is, of course, a Lowry,' he boasted.

He reached out with a gloved fingertip, almost caressing the painting. It was a river scene but not at all pretty, more like a wasteland – one you wouldn't want to walk through. Factories spewed out grey smoke. Not a person in sight, let alone an animal; it looked like the end of the world. It suited the Heron: grim and grey.

'I've received a message from Mr Samuels. He and your father are still off station,' he said, now standing in front of the large window, swatting away the buzzing fly.

Robyn sat forward eagerly in her chair. As she did so she noticed a familiar word written on one of the files on the desk. It was partly covered by another file, so she couldn't be certain, but it looked like *Doves*.

'Under ordinary circumstances, you and I would not be having this conversation. It falls to me to ask you to maintain the *situation* upstairs.' He sniffed. To him, what was going on upstairs wasn't worthy of the word *operation*. 'In the interim, which I'm sure will be a matter of hours, a day at worst, you will report all your activities to me . . .' He paused to squash the bustling fly against the window. As he smeared its body down the pane with his gloved finger, the room fell silent.

Robyn's head was spinning with far too much information. She opened her mouth to speak but he was talking again.

'In the short term, as I say, no more than a day, Mr Samuels has asked me to pass over operational control to . . . well, *you*, as there is no one else.'

'Where are my father and Mr Samuels?' she asked. She didn't want to reveal to him that she knew they'd gone to Windsor, or was it one of the other royal palaces? Maybe Sandringham? Either way, it didn't do to share with the Heron what she did and didn't know. They weren't supposed to talk to anyone 'outside' their area of work at the park, which meant no one had a clue what anyone else was doing.

He ignored her question anyway, gesturing to his overflowing trays of paper before walking around from his desk and holding open the door. She wanted to ask him about the file, which must be the one he had intercepted from the rider. But what could she say without giving herself away? She needed to get back to the loft and try to piece it all together. She made to step past him and leave the room, but he blocked the doorway with his body.

'I am sure I have no need to remind you of your solemn pledge?' he said, his spindly arm reaching across the doorframe.

'No,' she forced out, trying to keep her head up.

'You will, of course, disclose the nature of your work to no one. Any information shared, which could be of use to the enemy in ways you can't possibly imagine, is an act of *treason*. I am sure I have no need to remind you of the extreme penalties?'

'No,' she repeated. How dare he talk of treason when he was the one stealing secret files and measuring up creepy coffins?

'No, what?' He waited for her to admit he was in control, and she was nothing but a stupid schoolchild.

'No, *sir*.'

Yes, Robyn decided, as the Heron finally allowed her to leave, she hated him with an absolute passion. She was more determined than ever to catch him in the act, whatever the act might be.

But now she was going to run the pigeon operation overnight, which was terrifying and wonderful in equal measure. She'd have to sleep in the loft. Would it be too much to call herself Head of Operations for the National Pigeon Service, even if only for a matter of hours? Ned and Mary would be delighted with her promotion! They could stay in the loft with her. She'd need to make sure the pigeons were fed and watered and record their comings and goings in the logbook. She would *legitimately* be allowed to answer the telephone every single time it rang. And perhaps there would even be enough time to find out exactly what *Codename: Doves* was about. Without realising it, the Heron had handed her the key to unlock whatever secret he was keeping!

17

The first bomb punched the air from her chest, lifting her off her feet. The monstrous wail of the air-raid siren sounded its danger warning. Something shattered outside. A high-pitched whistle filled her ears. The second deafening bomb found its target, sending vibrations through her whole body. She screamed as the room shook and then she was on her back. As she looked up through a window, it shattered. The unmistakable *whirr whirr* signalled the arrival of a third bomb, which fell with force. A great column of black smoke rose into the night sky. She righted herself but fell again, in pain; something was wrong with her legs or feet. She crawled to Joy's hutch, which she'd moved to the quietest corner of the loft as instructed. She held out her shaking hand, but Joy wouldn't come.

'Joy. *Come, come, come.* Joy?' Her voice cracked. 'Joy, come on, come out. *Please?*' she begged. But Joy wasn't moving. 'We need to get out of here.'

A plane rumbled overhead. It felt like the building was

being squeezed and shaken as deafening thuds came from outside. Robyn reached her hands into the hutch and wrapped them around Joy's body, pulling her out. To her relief, she could feel Joy's heart beating. Mr Samuels had told her that pigeons' hearts beat six hundred times a minute – but right now it was much slower than that, and Joy was very cold. It must be the shock. If she could get Joy home, her mother would know what to do. Bletchley Park was being bombed – *she* was being bombed. This wasn't an attack happening miles away in London or Edinburgh. She wasn't hearing about this second-hand on the wireless or shielding herself from the front pages of her father's newspaper. This was her home, and it was under attack, even though her father had promised the park was not a target; his promises were being blown to smithereens all around her.

She stopped breathing for a second and smelt the air, checking for gas – not that she knew how to identify it. She was sure that she'd have heard a signal from the warden if it was gas. Should she dampen a sheet and put it over her mouth and Joy's beak? The all-clear sounded once, followed by a second of silence, which was then replaced by shouting. The church bells weren't ringing so it couldn't be an invasion. She wasn't sure if the bells were even still in place at St Mary's. Hadn't her father said they'd been taken and melted down? What was the code word on the radio for an invasion? Was it *Cromwell*? The pigeons were calling to her in agitation, wanting reassurance, but she had to think of Joy.

'I'll come back for the rest of you as soon as I can,' she promised.

Crawling to the door, she cradled Joy, bracing herself to stand up and face whatever was out there. Battered buildings and broken bodies? She tucked Joy inside her overalls and pushed open the door to the loft. Placing one foot tentatively in front of the other, she realised her boots were gone. Could they have been blown off? She didn't have time to go back and search for them, so she inched her way along the landing in her socks, which were wet. She leant over the thick oak banister, glad the staircase was still there. She could hear a commotion downstairs. People were charging around in all directions, issuing instructions. Robyn watched them running in and out of the Mansion, only moving when Joy released a shuddery breath.

'All right, Joy. Let's get you home.'

She held her arms across her chest to keep the bird in place as she painfully descended the stairs. Outside, murky smoke filled the air. Beams of light crossed paths, coming from torches held by faceless strangers in the dark. A searchlight shone on a small group of workers gathered around a hefty tree that had fallen in front of the lake. Some were bleeding but standing, unsteady on their feet. Most were moving towards one of the wooden huts. A strange silence surrounded them in the darkness. Like a sheep, she followed the crowd, tripping on a pothole in the drive, disorientated. She couldn't remember where to put her feet; it was bewildering and painful without her boots. She held Joy to her chest, then reached into her pocket for her torch. She pumped it several times with her free hand then shone it on the ground to light her way.

Through the big gates, beyond the damaged hut, a fire was raging. St Mary's Church had been hit. A Jeep was parked facing the gates with its diffused headlights on. The men gathered around the edges of the ruined building. Robyn stepped forward to watch them for a moment as they tried to put out the fire. For once, Robyn was glad that Mary and Ned were far away from her and the park, tucked up in their beds by now.

'Is anyone badly hurt?' a voice called out urgently but with authority.

'I don't think so, Claire. There were people inside but . . . I'm not sure,' replied a dazed man, rubbing his bleeding face.

'Let's take a roll call to make sure,' Claire replied, grabbing a pen and a notepad from her handbag.

The workers from the hut sat about on the lawn, a grey veneer of dust and ashes coating their shocked faces. Robyn saw a first-aider hand out paper towels and bandages. The man with blood on his face held his arm up, wincing in pain. A large shard of glass was sticking out of it.

'Let's get that cleaned up, shall we? Looks like it just missed an artery! You are lucky, Andrew!' the first-aider joked, earning a weak smile in reply.

'Are there any fatalities?' Claire asked the woman next to her, flicking her long hair out of the way.

'Not that I know of,' the woman said with relief.

'Goodness, you've lost your shoes. Are you hurt?' Claire said, noticing Robyn for the first time. 'Annabelle, look, her feet are bleeding,' she said to the other woman.

'It'll be from the glass,' Annabelle replied, looking at Robyn with concern.

'Have you seen my mother?' Robyn said. Right now, she couldn't care less about her feet or her boots. 'She runs the coffee hut – Wyn Lewis.'

'You ought to come inside with us. Lilia, get her a cup of sweet tea, would you?' Claire turned to another first-aider.

'Oh! What's that?' The first-aider pointed at Robyn's chest.

Claire reached out an arm as if to stop her. 'Hang on, there's something in there. Lilia, come and look, will you –'

'Wait! Come back! You might need medical attention!' Lilia called to Robyn as she got to her feet.

'I've got to go!' Robyn couldn't even begin to explain why she had a pigeon stuffed up her jumper.

The Heron had made it clear that she was to keep her mouth shut about the pigeons in the loft. Turning away from the women, the bombed hut and all the adults, she ran. She held Joy tight to her chest, grateful for the softness of the damp lawn. She would not let Joy become a casualty of the enemy's bombs. If Mr Samuels and her father returned home – *when* they returned home – it would not be to hear about the death of the best flyer at Bletchley Park. Not on her watch.

18

Robyn's mother wasn't in the cottage when she tore into the kitchen clutching Joy. Everything was in chaos tonight and no one was in their rightful place. The note she'd written, explaining her orders to sleep in the loft, sat untouched on the kitchen table.

'I don't think she's even seen it yet,' she told Joy. 'Where is my father? Surely someone knows where he and Mr Samuels have gone. This is exactly why people shouldn't keep secrets!'

She could only imagine that her mother had run to the Mansion when the bombs fell. She would have been helping people, lending a hand to clear up the damage. It was so difficult to try to second-guess where her mother was and what she might have done and how she might have acted. It wasn't as if they'd had training for this eventuality. She'd had no lectures about bombing from her mother or father because they'd both said it would 'never happen, not out here in the middle of nowhere with nothing to interest the enemy but sheep and fields!' But she knew, deep down, that no matter what bombs fell and what state her mother might be in, she wouldn't have stopped until she found Robyn. But that meant that she could have been in her coffee hut, close to where the bomb went off.

'No, no. *No!*' She shook herself, trying to dislodge the image of her mother's body lying lifeless.

If her father had been here, he'd have told her to stay put in the cottage. There'd have been no question of her going out so late. But he wasn't here.

'He's of no use to us when we need him, is he?' she said, cradling Joy as she walked into the scullery. 'He should have told me where he was going!'

One-handed, she dragged a sheet off the wringer and covered the Belfast sink with it, making a bird bed. She tucked Joy in and closed the window, then tucked the rest of the sheet over the pigeon.

'Will you be warm enough?' Robyn wondered aloud, turning to grab a few towels before adding them to the makeshift bed.

Mr Samuels had told her that pigeons can't see in the dark. She lit an oil lamp, which set a soft glow around the scullery. That would be a comfort to Joy.

'I'll be back as soon as I can. *Back in a flash*, isn't that what Mary says?' Her voice was calmer now. She always felt better when she was doing something practical.

Robyn shut the back door to the cottage and grabbed a pair of wellingtons from the rack, as she had no boots to wear. She winced as she pulled them on over her cut and bloodied feet, then set off, shutting the door behind her. In the courtyard she stopped for a minute, outside Mr Knox's cottage. She wanted to hammer on his door and ask him or the Bow Tie to come and help her. But there were no lights on – if they were on station, they'd already be up and out. She ran on past, keeping her head down and slipping on the cobbles. It must have rained while she was inside with Joy.

There were still plenty of people in the distance. Torchlight came from all corners, lighting up the bombsite. As she crossed the courtyard, her eyes began to adjust to the dark. An odd shape formed, next to the stable door, yards from Mr Knox's cottage. It looked like a rounders bat, long and grey. But something about it didn't look right, she thought, approaching the object with caution. She stood right next to it in the dark, pumping her torch to shine a light. Then she finally understood what she was looking at – it was a bomb: an incendiary bomb.

They'd had a police lecture from WPC Lawrence in the main hall at school. She'd warned them not to pick up any objects that looked like enormous pens because they might be bombs. Robyn had seen plenty of bombs in the newsreels at the cinema in town and in the helpful booklet she'd stolen from the scullery. She'd always assumed the chances of finding one at Bletchley were slim. Yet here she was, steps from her cottage, looking right at a bomb. Rule No. 4 from *What to Do in Any Wartime Emergency* came to her as the rain started to fall.

'Learn the very simple and efficient measures for dealing with incendiary bombs and with incipient fires generally.'

Well, it wasn't on fire. Did that mean it hadn't gone off?

Would it go off now, right next to her, and kill her? And if it hadn't gone off yet, what was she supposed to do about it? What did the book say? *What did it say?* She frantically tapped at each of her pockets. Thank goodness Mr Samuels had given her such a sensible outfit. Bottom right, on the thigh, she found the small booklet. She pulled it out, shielding it to stop it getting wet. But that was no use because she needed to hold the torch to see what it said. She kicked open the door of the stable nearest to her and snuck inside. Then she set the book on the cold cobbled floor and pumped the torch as she re-read rule four.

'How to deal with incendiary bombs and household fires,' Robyn read aloud.

'"In civil defence, everybody has a part to play". . . Yes, yes, but what do *I* do? Come on! Right, the firebomb. Now we're getting somewhere,' she told herself, needing the comfort of a human voice, even just her own.

'"It may not explode at all". . . *Yes, yes*, and then what? "Act quickly!" But what does that actually mean?' She'd been hoping for a simple set of instructions. She put the torch on the floor, closed the booklet and put it back in her pocket.

She collected the torch. Remembering that she'd need to power it, she pumped it continuously in her hand as she approached the bomb.

'It's not on fire, it doesn't look like it's gone off, so . . . I should leave it and find an adult? Let them deal with it, shouldn't I?' She talked herself through her next steps.

'Or should I pick it up and throw it somewhere, out into the park and away from the Mansion and the huts?

Or maybe it's like a firework and I shouldn't touch it at all because it might burn me.'

She needed to decide and act on her decision – the lives of everyone at the park might depend on her. Stepping forward, she nudged the bomb with the toe of her wellington. She remembered the brief training session WPC Lawrence had run at school, showing them what a bomb looked like. But that had felt like fun, and she'd spent most of the time pulling faces at Mary and Sarah-Ann; at that point, the war hadn't even really started, and it did feel like the adults were making a bit of a song and dance about things. But this bomb was not the same as that bomb: this bomb was *live*. She withdrew her foot and took several paces back. She waited, and when nothing happened she wrapped the cuffs of her overalls around her hands to protect them. She touched the bomb with the pads of her fingers, expecting a burning sensation, but it wasn't hot.

'It mustn't have gone off and that's good . . . but that's also bad, *really bad*.'

The booklet said the bomb should only weigh two pounds, the weight of Joy and Charity together. She could carry it, run and launch it into open space – Bletchley Park certainly had enough of that. But running with the bomb might detonate it. The booklet hadn't said anything about touching it, although it did mention drenching it. The only place with lots of water was the lake. But she was not going to send some of her animals to their deaths by throwing a bomb into their home. What about all the people in the Mansion and at the park? The workers in other huts and cottages and the gatekeepers and the gardeners and cleaners and cooks. And, of course, there were all the people on night shifts, working in places she hadn't even thought about; there were almost sixty acres of parkland, more than at Buckingham Palace, even. Plus, Bletchley had a maze, croquet lawns, woods, and orchards – there had to be a better way of dealing with this bomb. She needed to think!

Robyn was going to have to find an adult. She turned and ran out of the stables when she crashed right into someone in the darkness, sending her torch flying to the ground, where it immediately went out.

'Oh, thank God!' she shouted in relief as they both righted themselves. It was an adult!

'You? What are you doing out here?' the Heron demanded incredulously.

'What are *you* doing out here?' she repeated back, almost in shock.

'Me? I was checking on . . . never you mind! Account for yourself!' Her question had taken him by surprise, but he quickly regained control.

'I . . . I found a bomb,' she blurted out, hating him, but relieved to have found someone to help.

'Don't be ridiculous, girl! The raid is over. Go home to your parents!'

She stood rooted to the spot, staring at him. He was clean, she noticed, with not a speck on his grey suit, and he had papers in his hands. And he'd come from the direction of the railway station. Why was he down there and not up in the Mansion like everyone else? That must be why he wasn't covered in ash, soot and debris.

'Do as you're told, you silly child!' he shouted at her, before marching off at pace in the direction of the Mansion.

The Heron must have forgotten all about her father being off site. She knelt on the ground to pick up her torch, wondering if it was completely broken. There was a piece of paper on the floor. She looked up in the direction of the Heron, but he was long gone – he was fast, for an old man. He must have dropped the paper when they bumped into one another. She pumped the torch – it still worked! – and held it over the sheet of paper, but it was gobbledygook, complete nonsense, a mess of letters. Was it the language she and Mary had made up? It didn't look like either of their handwriting. Had the Heron written it? What did it mean?

Now was not the time to try to work it out. Instead she took a deep breath and folded the sheet of paper into one of her pockets. If he could take her papers and belongings then she could take his! And she had bigger things to worry about as she turned back to the bomb. It was made of a grey, concrete-like substance and had small holes around the top section, big enough to fit a pencil through. The hole at the top had been sealed with a shiny material: copper, lead or magnesium, she thought.

'So much for an adult helping me! I'll manage by myself.'

She pulled her sleeves down over her hands. The bomb felt smooth and cold through her overalls. She peeled back the material from one hand and stroked the end of the bomb, near the sheet-steel tail fins. It was green, almost the same shade as the Anderson shelter in their garden. She took a deep breath and, before she could stop herself, grabbed the bomb with both hands. Robyn jumped up and ran out of the courtyard in the direction of the woods. She had to get the bomb as far away from the Mansion as she could before it exploded.

19

'Robyn? What are you doing out here?' Her father's voice made her jump so badly that she nearly dropped the bomb. 'Why aren't you inside? It's not safe!'

'Dad? Oh, Dad! You're here! You're home,' she cried in relief, spotting Mr Samuels too.

There were no streetlights after dusk. Curtains were drawn, and every light and lantern switched off or blown out. All she could see were the headlights of a vehicle and the smoke still coming from the church in the distance.

'Are you hurt? Are you injured? We saw the fires and smoke from miles away. It's like Bonfire Night. Come here,' her father instructed from the shadows.

'I can't,' she said.

She was desperate to keep running and get as far away from them as possible. At the same time, the urge to hand the bomb to her father and head for home was overpowering.

'There was no one in the sentry hut by the main gates.

All hands on deck, I should think, but we can't get in at any of the entrances,' Mr Samuels explained.

'Fire engines have blocked the gates by the Mansion and the back gates too.' Her father carried on talking. 'We thought we'd try this side gate here but it's no good.' He rattled it in frustration.

'Why weren't you here when I needed you?' Robyn cried through the bars. 'Where have you been all this time?'

'*What?* Sandringham . . . Why?'

'I thought you'd gone to Windsor.'

'Something happened. Look, it doesn't matter now –'

'You were wrong! They bombed us! The noise was . . . I had to get Joy out. There were fires everywhere. One of the huts collapsed and I didn't know what to do and . . .' She couldn't continue.

'Do you know how many bombs fell? What's the damage? Is your mother all right?' Her father fired questions at her.

'I can't find her! You promised us. You said no one would bomb Bletchley! You said it would never happen!' Robyn shouted at him. 'You keep breaking your promises to me!'

'I'm sorry,' he started. 'I didn't think they would. None of us did,' he said, coming closer.

'Get back!' she warned them, holding the bomb up so they could see it. 'Stay back!'

'Dear Lord!' Mr Samuels said, spotting what she was holding.

'*Oh, hell!* Put it down on the ground, slowly now. That's it, set it there and then step away. Carefully, come to me, steady now. Birdy . . . Come to me, that's right,' her father directed.

She wanted to tell him everything she'd discovered about the bomb, but words failed her. The three of them were in the dark, the men on one side of the gate and she on the other, like in a silent movie. She could hear their breathing, low and heavy. Mr Samuels was coughing, the smoke thick and murky in the air. Her own breath was thin and reedy, her chest constricted and tight now she'd stopped running. *I don't have a bad chest!*

Her father inched towards her, as close as he could get. He pressed his body against the gates. His familiar big hands stretched out to her through the railings. She must have put the bomb down at some point, but she couldn't remember doing it. She still carried the weight of it, the cold in her fingers. Mr Samuels appeared with a rug. Her father threaded it through the gates and wrapped it around her as best he could.

'I've got you. I've got you. I won't let go,' he promised, pulling her closer to him.

He held her up, which was a relief because her legs had turned to jelly. Her whole body was shuddering and her teeth were chattering so much she'd bitten her tongue and could taste the iron tang of blood. The bomb was behind her now. Robyn didn't dare look at it, but she could feel the threat of its cold metal presence. She could have told her father to go away, to be safe, and leave her to deal with it, but instead they dealt with it together. At some point, Mr Samuels had gone. Later she heard the screech of brakes when he came back with the keys to the gate. Robyn couldn't let go of her father's hands and he couldn't let go of hers. Mr Samuels opened the gate and had to peel her from him. If she'd had the strength, she'd have resisted. Mr Samuels caught her as she fell backwards, passing her to her father as if she were made of porcelain. He carried her close to his chest, the same way she'd carried Joy, home.

20

Robyn's mother painstakingly cleaned out the splinters and shards of glass from her feet, then sat on a hard chair at her bedside. There she remained the whole night long, with a candle for company, while Robyn's father went back to the Mansion, to help the Home Guard fight the fire. The explosions had knocked the electricity out. One of the bombs had also hit a gas pipe. She knew her mother would be fretting about her coffee hut, even though she hadn't said a word about it. She had plenty to say about the need for Robyn to eat, sleep and drink, however.

In the middle of all the chaos, Robyn had somehow completely forgotten about Joy, and only remembered when her mother's screams came from the scullery. Her father returned the pigeon to the loft, promising Robyn that he would make sure Mr Samuels took the best care of her, while her mother scrubbed out the sink.

In the afternoon, her mother reluctantly left her bedside. She promised that she'd be back as soon as possible, and told Robyn she wasn't to move a muscle, let alone get out of bed. Her mother wanted to volunteer with the clean-up operation in the Mansion and hut.

With Mam gone, Robyn seized the opportunity to work on her father. She crept out of bed when she heard him return from assessing the damage to the loft with Mr Samuels. He placed a wooden chair at the foot of the stairs and sat on it.

Now Robyn bargained with him from the top of the stairs.

'There's nothing technically wrong with me, Dad. Dr Andrews looked me over and says I'm right as rain,' she called down the stairs.

'Dr Hughes said no such thing. You're suffering from shock, Birdy,' her father called back up.

'He prescribed a good stomp outdoors. Dr Hughes said it would be just the ticket,' she reminded him, creeping to the top of the stairs. 'Exactly what the doctor ordered.'

'Despite your best efforts to get yourself blown to smithereens last night, I suppose there isn't much more damage you can do.' Her father weakened, and she was sure she saw the hint of a smile.

'I thought I was helping people. I had to stop the bomb from going off. Not that anyone believes me. We could have died, Dad. You, me and Mr Samuels. We could have been blown to bits,' she added, her voice breaking.

'I know, Birdy, I do know, and you were very brave. Your mother and I are enormously proud of you and what you tried to do. For what it's worth, I think a German bomber who'd taken a bit of damage was trying to limp home after another raid. Could be he wanted to get rid of them or was aiming for the railway or the brickyard.' Her father tried to reassure her.

'Why the brickyard? And where did you and Mr Samuels go, all that time?'

'I told you last night, the lofts at Sandringham and Windsor.'

'Have the Royal Family got pigeons too? Did you see the king or queen? Someone said the king's coming here to visit, but I think it's just gossip. What would he want to come here for?'

'I'm going to check that pipe, so I won't be here to see if you nip out. You are to be back by tea. And whatever you do, Birdy, don't tell your mother!' her father stage-whispered, making her laugh. 'And please, try to stay safe. For me?'

Pink bricks sat waiting in tidy stacks next to the Mansion, a speedy delivery from the brickyard down the road. They'd probably replace all the wooden huts now. Robyn made her way down to the lake, trying not to inhale the smell coming from the broken gas pipe. The debris had been cleared away. St Mary's spire had stopped smoking, in part thanks to her mother and the other women. They had saved it from ruin while she ran around the park with an incendiary bomb. Ned and his father were already hard at work with a group of mechanics from her father's garage. They were mixing sand and pouring in hot water from small stoves dragged outside – there was a lot of argument about temperatures and things not *setting right*, whatever that meant. Some of the men were laying out the bricks and hoping for the best. Bits of string were keeping the first few rows in place. She wondered what time they'd started building and what had happened to all the furniture that had been in the hut. Now she thought about it, a wooden hut hadn't been the best plan. It was never going to shelter the people working in there safely.

As she walked past, Ned stopped to drink from his flask, steam streaming from his mouth and nose, and caught her eye. Robyn nodded, raising her gloved hand to wave. She wished Ned could down tools and talk to her. The three of them needed to discuss what had happened last night. Her hand went to the small pocket of the dungarees her mother had made her – she had to admit they were nicer than Mr Samuels' overalls – where she'd hidden the folded piece of paper the Heron had dropped. Luckily, she'd had time to rescue the paper from her pocket while her mother was out.

She waited on the deck of the landing stage until she heard the clock tower chime four. A robin squatting on a tree stump observed her as something scuttled in the damp soil under the curled cold leaves of a rhododendron. She found a fistful of sunflower seeds in her pocket and scattered them at her feet; if she was still enough, the robin would skulk over and have her fill and she could sketch the bird while it ate. But the cold made her sneeze, loudly, scaring the robin away. A pair of soot-black coots lifted their pale faces, registering their surprise before deciding to ignore her.

She hoped Ned or Mary would come soon. Mary might get a quick tea break and Ned's father might send him on an errand. They'd know to look for her here by the lake. They could puzzle out the piece of paper, with its strange squiggles and signs, together. Robyn had studied it several times herself but so far all she'd managed to read was *go*, *oil* and *sin*, which was of no use to anyone.

A sea-blue bloodless damselfly darted across the water, sharp and needle-fast and seemingly oblivious to the cold. Robyn wished she wasn't a mammal and could dive into the lake without worrying about the temperature. She stood facing away from the Mansion, and the bitter wind, turning her back on it to erase the images playing over and over like a cinefilm in her head.

The ding of a bicycle bell alerted her to Mary careering around the back of the lake. She looked unsteady as she bumped up and down in the saddle. She'd placed her satchel in the basket on the front of the bike and it was threatening to topple out. Behind her, Robyn heard Ned thundering down the frosty gravel path. She closed her eyes and thought about what she was going to say to them both. No one had told her not to speak about the bomb. She hadn't signed anything this time, so she didn't see why she couldn't tell her friends about what she'd done. It wouldn't feel real until she had.

'Are you all right?' Ned asked, puffing as he reached her. He put his hands on his knees. 'Ugh, I've got brick dust stuck in my throat.' He coughed, wiping his face on the sleeve of his jacket.

'You smell of soot. Are you going to rebuild the huts now?' she asked.

'Don't know. Lucky no one was seriously hurt.' Ned paused as Mary arrived.

'I heard some men from the Mansion say something about lack of protection from shrapnel. Did you hear the school was hit too?' Mary asked.

'No! *Our school?*' Robyn was horrified. Why had her parents kept that from her?

'Not yours. Elmer's School,' Ned explained. 'It's a private school, but no one was in it at that time of night. They say it was a stick of six bombs and they all fell in a line from St Mary's church to the hut.'

'Oh,' Robyn said with relief. 'I'm glad no one was inside.'

'Everyone's talking about it,' Mary said excitedly, pulling off her bobble hat. 'Security's tightened up even more.' She leant her bicycle against a Wellington tree and smoothed down her hair with her hands before re-tying the bands at the ends of her braids.

'Talking about it, are they?' Robyn snapped. 'Well, perhaps they shouldn't be. No one likes a gossip, Mary! You've spent too long at Mrs Fisher's!'

'It's hardly gossip, is it? It's all over town,' Mary said, sounding thrilled.

'Doesn't mean you should be adding to it!' Robyn shouted, surprising herself as well as her friends. She'd never shouted at either of them before. They were both new friends really, and she wasn't fully confident that they'd forgive her.

Ned quickly pulled something from his pocket and gave it to her, breaking the tension.

'What is it?' she said gruffly, still smarting from Mary's tactless comments.

'Something I made for you, until you're allowed your own boat back. Call it a late birthday present, if you like?' he offered.

'Next year we'll have a tea party, here, by the lake,' Mary suggested, with an offering of peace in her voice. 'We could make a campfire and toast marshmallows to make up for this year being so rotten. Open it, then.'

Still avoiding Mary's gaze, Robyn took off her gloves and tore the brown paper apart to reveal a small wooden boat.

'Oh, that's beautiful, Ned. Did you . . . did you make it yourself?' she asked, her annoyance with Mary dissolving.

'Yes. I made the bow and stern from bits and pieces lying around my father's workshop. I'm sure he won't miss them.'

'Finders keepers,' Mary said supportively, smiling broadly at Robyn.

'It's not my best effort. I only just started learning to varnish,' Ned explained.

Robyn held the boat in the palm of her hand. There were one or two bits of sawdust on the stern, which must have stuck to the varnish.

'It's brilliant. I love it. I can't wait to try it out on the water,' she said, and for the first time she forgot about last night.

'Let's float it on the lake,' said Mary. 'Then you can tell us all about the bombs! I was hoping you'd both be down here. So, at first, I thought it was the fast train to Scotland. You know how that shakes the houses in town, Ned? Anyway, you could hear the bombs going off from Mrs Fisher's. When I ran out, I could smell it. It must have been . . .' Mary rattled on.

'*Shut up, Mary!* Just stop going on and on! Look, *I* found one of the bombs! It was by the stables. I didn't know what to do. I was going to get help. Then the Heron turned up. He didn't believe me. He left me to deal with it. I had to pick it up and then . . .' Robyn burst into tears.

She felt angry that this had happened to her and everyone at the park. And she didn't have the words right now to explain it to her friends. But all Mary seemed to be able to think about was what a good story it would make, even though it wasn't a story, it was real, and it had happened right here. To her.

'Sorry, Robyn, you should have said.' Mary reached out to her, but Robyn shook her off. She didn't want anyone to touch her.

'*You found a bomb?*' Ned asked, moving closer. Robyn backed away from him too, standing on her gloves.

'What did you do with it?' Mary asked, incredulous, walking towards her again, as if to hug her.

'My father and Mr Samuels . . . They took it but . . . I don't want to talk about it,' she said, shoving both Mary and Ned away from her. She pushed Ned harder than she intended and he lost his balance and fell over.

'Robyn! What's wrong? Come back!' Mary shouted. 'Robyn! Don't be daft!'

Robyn ran to the end of the landing stage and jumped into her boat, pushing off from the frozen bank.

'*Robyn!* You're being an idiot. What's got into you?' Mary called after her in shock.

She didn't turn around; she didn't wait to hear if Ned would call her too. She'd shoved him so roughly he'd probably cut himself landing on the stones and gravel. She had been going to show them the Heron's mysterious piece of paper. She had meant to tell them about how she had saved Bletchley Park from a bomb. But it had all gone wrong. She set Ned's present down in her boat and rowed hard through the water, away from her friends.

21

'Robyn! Wait. Stay there!' Ned called out.

'Where else is she going to go?' Mary laughed and, despite herself, Robyn laughed too, even as she moved away from shore. 'It's not like she can row out to sea, is it?'

'We're coming!' Ned shouted clambering into a boat. 'Just stop rowing so bloomin' fast or we won't be able to catch you up. Mary's not as good a rower as you are!'

Robyn smiled a wobbly smile, put the oars down and turned around. It was freezing cold, and she wished she hadn't left her gloves behind. Once they were all on the island, hidden from sight, she'd show her friends the Heron's piece of paper, to make up for flouncing off. It had to have something to do with *Codename: Doves*. Together, especially with Mary's help, they'd be able to puzzle it out.

Robyn looked over to where she expected the boat carrying Mary and Ned to appear. But then –

'*Arghh!*' The shocked cry was followed by a splash.

'Ned!' Mary screamed.

Mary tried to stand up in the boat, pointing at the lake. 'He . . . he fell in!'

'Sit down,' Robyn told Mary, 'otherwise you'll fall in too!'

Robyn shrugged off her coat and dived into the water. There was no time to kick off her plimsolls. She surfaced already swimming in the direction of Mary's boat. There was no sign of Ned. No arms or hands thrashing up to the surface. No head bobbing to take a quick gasp before disappearing back under the water.

'*Here!* He was here!' Mary shouted, pointing ahead of the prow of the boat.

Robyn pulled herself through the peaty water, trailing pondweed and yellowing water lilies.

'Ned!' she managed to squeeze out as she neared Mary's boat, but there was no reply. 'Get help,' she blurted out, then gulped in as much air as possible before diving back down again.

She had to find him, and fast. How long had he been under? It could only be seconds, not even a minute. She dived down with her eyes wide open, searching. The bed of the lake bubbled with life, fish, plants, stones, a few coins – but no Ned. She whirled around in the opposite direction. *Where was he?* She spun around in a full circle, treading water. Minnow-fast, she swam around the area where Mary had pointed. The shadow of Mary's boat inched back towards the landing stage. Help would come, but not in time. She had to do something *now*! She surged through the water, looking everywhere she could. Then she saw a shape in the water. She swam towards it. It had to be Ned!

As she reached him, she could see he wasn't moving. She grabbed the back of his jacket and turned him to face her. His eyes and mouth were closed. Blood seeped into the water like a thread of red cotton, spooling from his head. Robyn wrapped herself around him, cupping her hands underneath his armpits. She dragged him up to the surface, his weight fighting her every inch of the way. Then she tilted backwards and pulled him onto her chest, just how her father had shown her when he first taught her to swim. She prayed that she'd have the strength to kick them back to her boat. She tilted her head and Ned's out of the water, her hand holding his chin up. She could feel his pulse.

A murder of coal-black crows cried, circling the commotion in the water. Her boat hadn't drifted far from where she'd left it. Without loosening her grip on Ned, she kicked them towards it. She placed his arms over the edge of the boat and let herself sink underneath him into the water, then she launched him with her shoulders awkwardly upwards. She dragged her arms across the oar hook and managed to pull herself fully inside too, the hook tearing her skin as she fell onto her belly. She didn't allow herself a moment to rest but rowed automatically, back to the landing stage.

Help was coming. She could see adults running across the lawn from the Mansion. She hoped she'd done enough to save Ned. His pulse had been very weak in the water, but as her boat hit the landing stage, Robyn could see his chest moving up and down. He was alive.

22

December 1939

'We're going to have an open-door policy this Christmas,' her mother said.

'For all the chaps who can't get home,' her father explained as he passed Robyn a hot chocolate. It was Nestlé milk! She wasn't usually allowed it, but since the *incident in the lake*, as he was calling it, her father had started paying attention to her, offering her treats when he could. He'd told her how proud he was that she'd jumped in to save Ned. Mary said she deserved a medal. Ned said nothing as she hadn't seen him since that day. Mary had, though, and reported that Ned was as well as could be expected but was on bed rest. Doctor's orders.

When she returned to the loft, Mr Samuels had kept Robyn occupied with pigeon-related tasks. She had barely seen Mary, who had suddenly become terribly busy, with a flurry of messages needing to be delivered to Mr Knox's cottage. There was something going on in there – Mr Knox and the ladies had an air of excitement and, at other times, desperation. Mr Letton drove in and out of the park in the hearse each day, but without Ned in the passenger seat. However, as Mary told Robyn in the snatched moments where they passed each other outside the cottages, there was always hope.

'Can't we invite Mr Knox and the ladies instead?' Robyn replied, rousing herself from her thoughts. She'd far rather spend the evening chatting with the Bow Tie than lots of dull old suits. 'Oh! Can Mary come? And maybe Ned? We haven't even seen Ned since . . .'

'We'll see,' her mother said. 'She's right, though, Vern, it's not only the chaps, is it? There're girls stuck here over the season too. Could you get me some more eggs, please, Robyn? I've a sponge to bake. Vern, did you get the plum gin from the shed?'

'I'll get it!' Robyn offered, remembering the *borrowed* tyre she'd stashed there.

She'd been planning to make a tree swing today for Ned and Mary, to make up for her poor behaviour, but hadn't had the chance yet. Robyn had been helping her parents all morning. She'd squeezed in a few precious hours with Mr Samuels, Joy and the birds before the clock chimed four. Now she had one hour until Sunday teatime. Mr and Mrs Samuels would be joining them today. Mr Samuels and her father were now as thick as thieves, after their adventure *off station*. Both men were being very cagey, despite her best efforts to find out what they'd been up to at the royal palaces.

She sat on the cobbles, pulling on her plimsolls, which still smelt of the lake. The horse chestnut trees were bare but for the sticky buds. Leaves layered the garden, in different states of decay. As she shivered in the frost, Robyn pulled a scrap of paper out of her pocket and jotted down a few words. *Meet me at the lake. I've got a surprise for you.* She folded the paper and scrawled Mary's name on it then ran around to Mr Knox's front door and shoved it through his letterbox. One of the ladies in the cottage would pass it on to Mary when she came to deliver the mail. Robyn darted around the back of her cottage to the shed. Should she bring one bottle of gin or two? She didn't want her mother coming back to get another one, so better grab two, she decided. She left them by the back door next to the empty milk bottles. A shuffling in the trees told her the blue tits had someone on watch duty.

Robyn arrived at the lake, half-wheeling, half-carrying the tyre. She was both delighted and surprised to spot Ned on the landing stage instead of Mary. He was hopping from foot to foot, wrapped up from head to toe. She was so relieved to see him at last, as well as nervous. She didn't know what to say to him, how to even begin to apologise for what had happened. She'd half expected his father to ban him from ever returning to Bletchley.

'How did you know I'd be here?' she asked, testing out a smile on him. Would he still want to be her friend? He might not even talk to her.

'Where else would you be?' He smiled.

'Glad to see you're alive and kicking, although you look like you're about to set off to the North Pole!' she said pointing at his balaclava, scarf, gloves, snow boots and duffle coat.

'I've been in bed forever, smothered by blankets and fuss for weeks. I can't believe I missed Bonfire Night!'

'Ah, you didn't miss much. Squibs and crackers – and in the day too. No guys, no fires, no nothing.' Robyn sighed. 'Everything's cancelled! I want life to go back to normal.'

'Me too. But there's always next year; we'll celebrate then. If my mother hadn't had to go down the brickyard, she'd have kept me in bed until Christmas. At least we've got that to look forward to. My father wanted her to take me with her to work, but she wouldn't for some reason.' Ned shrugged. 'Not that I'm complaining. I don't want to be stuck down the boring old brickyard when I could be here with you and Mary.'

'Mary and I were worried you might have caught pneumonia. You are all right, aren't you, really? I can't believe we haven't seen you for a whole month. Mary will be thrilled! I managed to slip a note for her through Mr Knox's door. I told her I was coming down here. If she gets a break, I'm sure she'll pop down on her bicycle. I was going to make a tree swing and surprise you both, but that doesn't matter. Tell me truly, are you better?'

'Doing well on all fronts,' Ned reported. 'Right as rain.' He coughed then flapped a hand to wave away her concern. 'I've got three vests on!'

'So, what happened?' Robyn dared to ask at last. She'd spent the last few weeks imagining every possible scenario.

'It was a pike. I've never seen one in real life and I panicked. It had these huge eyes and a horrible gaping mouth and rows of fangs. It looked like a shark about to attack me.'

'When have you ever seen a shark, Ned Letton?' she asked, trying to lighten the mood.

'In books, at school. Either way, I am never ever going back in that lake again,' Ned vowed. He rubbed at a faint scar on his temple. 'I had a right old egg on my head. Didn't go down for at least a week. Mum says I looked a fright. Wouldn't let me out of her sight.'

'Well, the egg's gone now. Pikes are terrifying. My father calls them water wolves.'

'I can see why!'

'I'm so glad you're here. We've been watching for you, ever since that day. I did wonder if your father might never let you back. Thank goodness your mum got a job! Anyway, your timing's perfect. Mam says it's going to snow.' Robyn pointed at the white sky, heavy with promise.

'But it won't be the same as snow days at school though, will it?'

'Don't tell me you're missing school?'

'No, not really. Well, maybe a little bit,' Ned admitted.

'I'll make a snowman with you. And I'm a crack shot at snowballs,' she offered, wanting to cheer him up and move away from the memory of what happened in the lake.

Robyn decided she was going to set herself a challenge. She was going to make Ned's life happier and safer and repair the damage she'd done when she pushed him away from her. She was to blame for him nearly drowning.

'Why are they taking the aerials down, do you think?' Ned asked, pointing at the workers by the Mansion. So much had changed while he'd been gone.

'It's a bit of a giveaway from the air, isn't it? Besides, they're all on their last nerve, after we had our bob's worth of bombs.'

'Where's Mary?' he asked, looking around for a bicycle heading their way.

'Dunno. Maybe she didn't get my note. Let's not wait. Why don't we make a start?' Robyn hefted the tyre off the ground and looked around for the best tree.

'All right. As long as I can have the first go!'

The tree swing was soon set up and Robyn checked she'd knotted the rope as securely as possible. Much to Ned's disgust, she tested the swing herself first. She couldn't bear the weight of another accident on her conscience.

When the lake thawed and the temperature warmed up, which wouldn't be until May, she was going to teach Ned to swim. And she would have the patience of an angel and not get cross with him at all, she resolved. Right now, she forced herself to have the patience to wait for Mary to turn up; she was desperate to tell both her friends what was on the piece of paper the Heron dropped.

'I'd suggest taking you skating on the lake, now it's frozen, but I don't think that would go down too well with your parents.' She smiled.

'I told you, I'm not going on that lake ever again!' Ned reminded her. 'It's already perishing. My flannel was frozen when I went to wash my face this morning. Have you got skates, then?'

'I've got an old pair, but I doubt Mary will have any – where is she, anyway?'

'At last! About time!' Robyn shouted on hearing Mary's bicycle bell and she jumped off the swing in mid-air. 'I've got something to tell you about the night of the bombing,' she told Mary.

'What? Why didn't you show me?' Ned asked, sounding hurt.

'I wanted to wait until we were all together again. Three heads are better than one. Or two. No offence, Ned.'

Robyn showed them the piece of paper. It had dried out now, but the ink was blurred and the edges had frayed. The three of them stood in silence for a moment, trying to digest the word puzzle facing them.

'It's my fault. If I hadn't fallen in . . .' Ned looked desperate.

'Don't be daft. It's my fault for huffing off,' Robyn reassured him.

'Can't you remember any of the letters or words?' Mary asked.

'No. I thought I saw the words *go*, *oil* and *sin*, but I could be wrong.'

'It's like trying to do a jigsaw without the picture on the box,' Mary nodded.

'But if there's one piece of paper with coded messages on –' Ned said.

'Of course! There must be others, and we have to find them!' Mary said.

'If he's made one mistake, he'll make another,' Ned said.

'With the three of us back together, we'll be right there, on the spot, when he does,' Robyn said, smiling at her two best friends.

23

'How was the big meal with Mr and Mrs Samuels?' Ned asked, as he sat down on the fallen log next to Robyn.

She was surprised he'd remembered. 'Long! Adults really like to talk. But it ended better than I thought it would.'

'What's this?' Mary said, leaning her bicycle against an oak tree.

'Robyn's boss came for tea last night,' Ned filled her in. 'And something good happened.'

'What?' Mary joined them on the log.

They'd decided yesterday that the lake was too public a place to conduct their covert operations and had agreed to start meeting in the woods every morning for their tea break. They had to get to the bottom of the Heron's suspicious activities, and now they were reunited there was no time to waste. It could be a matter of national urgency.

'Mr Samuels made me responsible for Joy during the breeding programme,' Robyn told the other two.

'Ugh!' Mary screwed up her face. 'I don't want to hear about pigeons making babies.'

'Well done, Robyn,' Ned interrupted.

'Oh yes, I mean, well done you, and all that,' Mary hastily added. 'I know *you* like them, but it's not as if you can cuddle them like you can a pet, is it?'

'Shut up, Mary. Tell us more,' Ned said.

'I've got to watch Joy's calcium and mineral intake, and make sure everything she has is nutritious. Then, if I do my job right, Joy will lay her eggs. Then there's an incubation period, which I'm in charge of. After that the squabs – that's the babies – will be my responsibility too.'

'*Squabs* is a funny word, isn't it?' Ned said. 'Sounds like they'd be forever bickering and fighting, like my brothers, Rob and Joe were. Before, you know . . .' Ned tailed off.

'It is a funny word. Mr Samuels calls them squeakers too. Did you know that, in the wild, both the mum and the dad pigeon can feed the babies? Isn't that clever! They make milk, in their crop – a neat pouch under their beaks. And then they regurgitate it –'

'That is the most disgusting thing I've ever heard!' Mary looked and sounded repulsed. 'Wouldn't you prefer to be a messenger girl?'

'No! Don't you think nature is clever? Anyway, Joy's squabs are professional pigeons and they're mine until they get their feathers and then Joy will teach them to fly. And then they'll be off . . .' She stopped because she didn't like the next part of Mr Samuels' plan. 'Fledged.'

'You fell on your feet with Mr Samuels, didn't you? All

159

I'm good for is running errands.' Ned looked fed up. 'Did I tell you I saw the Heron in the newsagent's?'

'No! What was he doing? Anything suspicious?' Robyn instantly forgot all about the squabs.

'Not really, but he almost got into a row with Mr Arlo. He gave the Heron a right going-over about not being *part of the war effort* and *why wasn't he in uniform?*'

'Oooh. I'll bet the Heron didn't like that! What did he say?' Mary grinned.

'Nothing. Not a word. Just dropped his newspaper on the counter and stormed out.'

'Blimey. No wonder he's always in such a temper if that's how he's treated. I thought he'd be too old to join up and that's why he's working here,' Robyn mused. 'Gosh, I miss going into Mr Arlo's to get my sweets.'

'I'll get you some, quick too, before they ration them!' Ned joked.

'It's not so much the sweets I miss, to be honest, it's more being allowed to scoot down there on my bicycle and get them for myself. I can't remember the last time I left this place.'

She realised that she was being a moaning Minnie, but it had already been an age since she left the park, and some days it was all a bit too much. It was different for Mary and Ned: they could come and go as they pleased. She, on the other hand, really was trapped.

'Maybe the Heron's not as old as we thought he was,' suggested Mary. 'I don't know – they all look the same to me, the men at the park. All smart suits and stuffy ways, looking down their nose at me.'

'Apart from Mr Knox?' Robyn checked.

'Oh yes, he's one of a kind. Says he'd rather work with women any day of the week! Doesn't bat an eyelid when the Bow Tie smokes her pipe. She told me that Mr Knox had a proper stand-up row with top brass over the ladies' pay. Wants it to be equal – can you believe it?' Mary shook her head.

'Wish I could work with Mr Knox, instead of my father. I'm so sick of measuring. It's like being back at school.' Ned sighed.

'What are you measuring?' she asked.

'Coffins. Planks of wood. And I had to find out how long the hearse is if you remove the back seats.'

'Sounds desperate.' Mary sympathised.

'Ned!' Robyn exclaimed. 'Don't you think that if the Heron's asked your father to sneak something out of the park in the hearse, then it can't be paperwork? It must be something big! And if it's not a body, then what is it?'

'Please don't let it be a body!' Mary said.

'Let's rack our brains for something large at Bletchley Park. Large and important enough that the enemy would want to get their hands on it,' Robyn suggested.

'Do you think it's something hidden in the huts? From what I've seen around the park, it's just maps and typewriters. Desks and all that,' Mary said.

'*Could* it be an actual dead body?' Ned said tentatively. 'Should we tell someone?'

'But what would we tell them? We haven't got any proof. Besides, who's going to believe us?' Robyn shook her head.

'And it's not like anyone's gone missing, is it?' Ned said.

'Actually . . .' Mary started, then stopped.

The three of them looked around the woods as a branch cracked in the distance, followed by voices.

'*Shush. There are people talking. Listen* . . .' Robyn mouthed then held a finger up to her lips.

'. . . as well you know, having signed the act yourself. It's not as if we can ask her directly. It falls to you to resolve the situation. And resolve it you must or face the direst consequences.'

'Is that the Heron?' Robyn whispered to Ned and Mary. The three of them froze on the log. The last thing they needed was for him to find them in the woods.

'*Who is he talking to?*' Robyn mouthed. Ned and Mary both shrugged.

'We cannot allow members of the public, and especially not a *writer*, to bring into question anything that happens here at the park.'

His authoritative voice was now unmistakable. It seemed to be coming from deeper inside the woods.

'We should run,' Ned whispered, getting to his feet. But Robyn grabbed his arm and shook her head.

'*Stay still and low,*' she mouthed to Ned and Mary as the Heron's voice grew louder.

The three of them ducked and kept as still as they could.

'But she doesn't know what we're doing here,' another voice said.

Mary mouthed, '*It's Mr Knox!*' She looked both surprised and worried.

Robyn understood why. It wouldn't do if Mary's boss

found her skipping work in the woods, and her tea break had probably ended ages ago.

'What on earth are they doing skulking about in the woods?' Ned began.

Robyn held up a hand to silence him. He was going to give them away if he didn't shut up!

'Come on, man! You must see that naming a character Major Bletchley could be a message or a sign to someone?' The Heron raised his voice in anger.

'You don't think that *I* –' Mr Knox replied crossly.

'I do indeed, and Whitehall have charged me with interviewing you. Which is why we're out here. This war is about to enter an acute phase. I can assure you that we will spare no effort to secure victory.'

'I will not stand here and be interrogated by –'

'You will do as you're told. Meet with her.'

'*Here?*'

'Don't be a fool, Knox. Of course not here.'

'*Who are they on about?*' Ned mouthed.

Robyn shrugged.

'Where, then?'

'Invite her to your home at Courns Wood for afternoon tea and scones! Show her round your precious library, for all I damn well care –'

'How do you know I have a library?' Mr Knox interrupted.

'I know *everything*. Find out what she suspects, without giving away any more than you already have.'

'On my honour, I have given nothing away. Even my wife doesn't know what I do here. I can assure you . . .'

163

'I don't want your assurances. I want to know what Agatha Christie knows. And why the *bally hell* she put a character called Major Bletchley into a book about spies during a blasted war! For God's sake, man, what was she thinking? Tell her plainly to keep her mouth shut!'

'*The* Agatha Christie?' Ned whispered in shock. Robyn reached forward and put her hand over Ned's mouth in frustration.

'I will not. She's a trusted friend and I would never speak to her like that. I will ask her politely, if you insist, but I'm quite sure she knows nothing about this place.'

'Make certain of it. Leave no stone unturned. In the interval, I am investigating *all* your contacts and colleagues. There are others here whose behaviour has attracted suspicion. You seem hell-bent on surrounding yourself with all kinds of foreign and *exotic* types. If I had my way . . . No matter. I bid you a good morning, sir.'

Mary's eyes filled with tears. Robyn understood why immediately. She reached out and pulled Mary into a hug.

'You're not a contact. He doesn't mean you,' she whispered, hoping it was true.

Ned shuffled along the log as quietly as he could to Mary, who was crying now. He wrapped his arms around them both. They sat in an awkward huddle, each wondering when it would be safe to speak or stir. The cracking of branches had ceased, suggesting that both men had left the woods, but none of them wanted to move, not yet.

'This is bad, all right,' said Robyn, 'but look, I've got an idea. My parents are having a New Year's Eve party and I'm allowed to invite you both. At least, I *think* I am. I'm sure it will be fine. Anyway, we're going to divide and conquer: Mary, you're going to get chatting with Mr Knox and see what you can find out. There's no way he's blabbed to *the* Agatha Christie. The Heron suspects him and the ladies. We need to know what's going on in their cottage and how it connects to the Heron.'

'And I could chat to the Bow Tie and the other ladies; see what they think of the Heron?' Mary perked up.

'Great idea! Ned, you can corner one of the dispatch riders. Mam's invited Sadie and a few of the others, as they're not able to go home for Christmas. They might know who the Heron is and why he's allowed to intercept Mr Knox's files and post. And . . .' She gulped before continuing, 'I'll watch the Heron, like a hawk.'

The Heron was a law unto himself – accusing Mr Knox of breaking the Official Secrets Act! *How dare he?* She had to deal with him, for Mary's sake, and Mr Knox's too, before things got out of control. And the party was perfect: it'd allow her to stop him from spearing his prey.

24

New Year's Eve 1939

New Year's Eve was Robyn's favourite night of the year. She liked to stay up late and watch her parents' guests becoming louder and sillier. But this year her mind was on other matters. Their little cottage was brimming with adults. Mr Samuels caught her eye across the packed room and smiled. He and Mr D were leaning against open the back door in silence, companionably sending spirals of smoke into the crisp night air. Her mother refused to let anyone smoke in their cottage, even Mr D. Mr Samuels tapped his watch with his finger and she smiled in response.

She was looking forward to helping him once Joy's squabs were born. They'd both been watching Joy around the clock; she only left the hatching pot to drink or eat before scurrying back to her eggs to keep them warm. Mr Samuels told Robyn she was doing a grand job with Joy, who was going to make an excellent mother.

Her parents had given in and allowed her to invite Ned and Mary to the party, as her mother said it would mean she could keep an eye on the three of them. Ned was helping a chatty dispatch rider to more tea. Robyn was sure he'd be able to guide the conversation towards the Heron. Ned's mother, Helen, was speaking to Robyn's in hushed tones as they set out mince pies sprinkled with sugar and a jug of cream. Robyn glanced about the room, as if she were looking for someone. She was pleased to see that Ned's dad, Mr Letton, hadn't come.

Meanwhile, her father placed several bottles of damson gin and two bottles of rhubarb gin on the table. He refilled the Lewises' best duck-egg blue bone-china teapot, inherited from Grandmother Pat. It took pride of place; large enough to pour at least twenty cups, she guessed. Her father swirled his hand in a gesture that meant *Do something, make yourself useful!* She grabbed a bottle of cordial her mother had made up from the leftover fruit and offered it to Mary. The Bow Tie was talking to Mary about being *on- and off-station*. Mary responded with a damning review of the variable state of billet accommodation. The Bow Tie listened sympathetically before steering the conversation towards the latest American fashions. Robyn offered around a plate of mince pies, waiting for her father to forget about her. She put down the plate on the table next to Ned, who immediately stuffed a whole mince pie into his mouth, which was impressive. Robyn positioned herself by the fire, ready to spot the Heron. She took out the now very crumpled piece of paper. The codes had mostly been washed away by the lake when she'd dived in after Ned.

While she waited for the Heron, another man had taken her eye. She watched as he refused all offers of food and drink from her parents. Instead, he took out his own supplies – a small milk bottle, a teacup, and a twist of sugar wrapped up in brown paper – and made himself a cup of tea. How resourceful, bringing your own sugar ration to a party. Robyn noticed how he assessed the room, taking in everything and everyone. He eventually sat down on the only available seat, which was the piano stool, next to her.

'Happy New Year,' he said, raising his cup. It was china with a tiny chain attached to the handle.

'Happy New Year to you too,' she said, scrunching the piece of paper as quietly as she could into her fist.

'Have you made any New Year's resolutions?' he asked, as if he'd been rehearsing a question in his head. 'Is that what you've got there?' He pointed to her hand.

'No. It's a mystery rather than a list,' she said, tucking her hand behind her back.

'Mysteries are my speciality. How do you do? I'm Alan. Alan Turing,' he said, offering his hand as if she were another adult. Robyn liked him already.

'Hello. I'm Robyn Lewis.' She shook the man's hand, checking to see if her parents were watching. Luckily they were busy.

The scrunched-up piece of paper fell into her lap as she withdrew her hand from Mr Turing's.

'Would you like me to take a look, Robyn Lewis?' He waved his hand at the paper.

'Why not? Can't do any harm,' she sighed, passing it over to him.

He studied the crumpled mess without comment.

'*Caves* and *gallery*,' he said, quickly and quietly.

'Oh. I thought *oil*, *sin* and *go*. But I don't understand what any of these words have to do with Code –'

'*Alan!* Come over here. Welchman and I want you to meet someone!' Mr Knox interrupted.

Mary was standing next to a *Welshman*? And Mr Knox, looking excited.

'Ah, I am discovered,' Alan said, regretfully handing back the creased paper. 'You ought to look after that, you know,' he suggested as he folded up his twist of sugar and tucked it back inside his jacket. '*Island*,' he added, picking up his cup before draining it.

'Pardon?'

'Alan!' Mr Knox called – rather impatiently, she thought. 'Come and meet this bright young thing!'

Mr Turing lingered one more moment. 'Those letters there, the blurred ones, could be *island*. But it's hard to say with the water damage. Good evening,' he said, leaving her to join Mr Knox and Mary. And the Welshman, whoever he was.

She took out *What to Do in Any Wartime Emergency* and carefully placed the crumpled paper in the middle of the booklet, hoping to flatten out the creases.

Her mother came over. She had just enough time to tuck the booklet away again.

'Are you coming to join in with the hokey-cokey?'

'Yes, in a bit,' she said.

'What did he say, then?' Her mother perched on the piano stool Mr Turing had vacated. 'The Prof?'

'*Who?*' She had thought his name was Alan. 'Nothing. Wait, why?' she asked, suspicious of her mother.

'No reason. He's an interesting person, that's all.'

'Is he?' Robyn sat up in her chair watching Mr Turing, the Prof! – chatting to Mr Knox and Mary, who looked delighted to be speaking to the *interesting person*.

'Who is he, then? And why's he so interesting?'

'Just another Cambridge boffin,' her mother said, trailing her *Evening in Paris* scent behind her as she walked away.

She watched as Alan and the Welshman listened closely to Mary. They were almost immediately interrupted by the Heron, who swooped in through the door and headed straight towards them. Alan shook hands with him, then put his cup back in his jacket pocket and dipped his head goodnight to Mary. Then Alan, the Heron and Mr Knox all walked out of the back door and into the night. The Heron was as slippery as an eel. Appearing from nowhere before vanishing.

Mary, left standing on her own, spotted Robyn and gave the smallest of shrugs. Before Robyn could cross the room to question her, the Bow Tie came along. She looped her arm through Mary's, guiding her to a chair. She must have seen how rude the Heron had been and wanted to distract her from it. He was the most infuriating man Robyn had met in her whole life! Strutting about as if he owned the place – and in her cottage too!

Well, that didn't matter, Robyn realised, as she crumpled the piece of paper tightly in her fist. Mr Turing had given her a lead! Those three words – *caves*, *gallery* and maybe *island* – didn't make any sense, but they were at least a start!

25

January 1940

Naked trees like skeletons hung with old man's beard made the shared garden look untidy and bare as Robyn walked around the back of their cottage to Mr Knox's kitchen. Her mother had sent her with leftover mince pies from the party. She tapped on the back door and waited but there was no answer.

Robyn was about to leave, intending to try again later, when someone came barrelling out of the cottage, leaving the door wide open and almost running into her.

'Watch where you're going, can't you! Wait . . . *You again?* What are you doing, larking about here?' the Heron demanded.

'Nothing . . . I'm not larking,' she faltered.

'You do rather a lot of nothing. Shouldn't you be looking

after pigeons instead of loitering in doorways?' he asked, but didn't wait for a response, setting off towards the Mansion.

Robyn stood for a moment, watching him sweep through the back gate. Why was he using the back door? He should have used the front door to the cottage, in full view of everyone working in the stable yard. If the front door was good enough for Mr Turing and the men working in the bungalow opposite, who according to Mary liked to pop over every now and then, then it should be good enough for the Heron. He most definitely shouldn't have been coming and going through the cottages' shared garden; he didn't live there! But where *did* he live? Hopefully he'd been billeted with someone as horrid as Mary's Mrs Fisher. Anyway, Robyn would think about all the sharp responses she could have given him later. She stepped hesitantly into Mr Knox's cottage.

'"The River Thames has frozen for the first time since 1888,"' the Bow Tie read from her newspaper.

'Never mind the weather! Is there mention of her forthcoming book in there or not?' Mr Knox asked impatiently as the Bow Tie shook out the reduced number of pages – reduced due to lack of paper rather than lack of news.

'They're in raptures anticipating its publication next year. "Agatha Christie is a national treasure . . ."' the Bow Tie tailed off, spotting Robyn in the kitchen.

'Ah! Mince pies! Wonderful! Put them down there, Robyn.' Mr Knox spoke far too loudly. 'Not all our joys are to be rationed,' he added.

Her parents had been worrying about rationing, but as far as she could tell it hadn't caused them too much bother yet.

'. . . And, oh dear . . .' The Bow Tie stopped reading.

'What?' Mr Knox asked, forgetting Robyn instantly.

'It might be nothing. He says he's seen part of an early review copy. He mentions "an impressive knowledge of spy tradecraft."' The Bow Tie paused again.

'Oh Lord!' Mr Knox gasped. 'This will never do. They'll think I've something to do with it, for certain.'

'And I don't mean to alarm you, Dilly, but there's more. "Sounds uncommonly like a code for the fifth column . . ."' the Bow Tie stopped reading. She shut the newspaper firmly then folded it as small as it would go and put it in the kindling basket by the fireplace.

'I'll see you to the door, dear?' She steered Robyn away from Mr Knox, who had dropped heavily into his chair. 'Tell your mother she's the best baker in Bletchley!' the Bow Tie said, closing the door in Robyn's face.

'What's the fifth column?' Robyn asked Mary and Ned later, in the plum shed. After overhearing Mr Knox and the Heron, they'd decided that the woods were now as unsafe as the lake. They really were running out of hiding places. Maybe they should start climbing the trees.

'Spies,' Mary sighed. 'Enemies of the state. Espionage.'

'Does the Heron think Mr Knox is a turncoat or a double agent?' Robyn said in disbelief. 'Just because his friend has written yet another book about murder. She must have written at least twenty!'

'But she's called one of the main characters after this place,' Ned said. 'Maybe she does know something?'

'Maybe we *all* know things we don't *know* we know,' Robyn replied. Her mind kept turning over the words *caves*, *gallery* and *island*. She twisted them every which way, in the hope they'd suddenly make sense.

'Are you on about those code words again? Couldn't the man at the party have got them wrong?' Ned wavered.

'No, he wasn't the sort to get things wrong. You know, *we* could have picked up information and we don't know its value, but *they* do,' she explained.

'I heard one of the women in the huts refused anaesthetic for an operation. She was so worried she'd end up blurting out the secrets she'd been keeping in her head. There are all kinds of rumours,' Mary agreed.

'But that's all they are, aren't they? Rumours?' Ned said. '*I* haven't heard any.'

'You wouldn't though, would you? You're working with your dad in the huts. You don't go into the Mansion or any of the other places where us workers are,' Mary explained.

'What have you seen, then? What's happened, Mary?' Robyn asked. Something had spooked her friend.

'I didn't tell you because . . . Well, we're not supposed to talk, are we?' Mary said, the fear in her voice growing. 'This whole place is probably bugged!'

'They can't have bugged Robyn's plum shed, Mary!' Ned laughed. 'I doubt there's listening devices in the compost.'

'Tell us what happened,' Robyn said, eyeing her bicycle and the puncture she still hadn't got around to repairing.

'I was going to tell you, but then the Heron and Mr Knox appeared in the woods and had their horrible row. Remember?' Mary sighed.

'I knew there was something you weren't telling us,' Ned said.

'Two girls went missing after a terrible to-do in the canteen and I haven't seen either of them since. Everyone's stopped talking about them,' Mary babbled on.

The wind whipped through the thin wooden panels of the plum shed.

'It's like . . . they never existed.'

'Slow down, start again.' Robyn shifted position. She'd been sitting on her leg and had pins and needles. There was limited space in the shed with three of them in there.

'A woman from one of the huts found out her fella was cheating on her with a girl from another hut. They had a row at breakfast about who he trusted more and what he'd told them.' Mary spoke fast. 'One of them threw a plate of prunes and toast at the other. There was a right scene.'

'Blimey!' Ned said. 'Is it normally like that in there?' His eyes widened.

'Was it because of rationing? My dad said that'll cause fights,' Robyn said knowledgeably. 'My mum heard a rumour that Mr Squires, the grocer, had some oranges. She wanted to send my dad into town as she wants to make marmalade.'

'No, it wasn't about rationing, Robyn. I mean, you're only allowed one slice of toast now and no second helpings but it's very relaxed usually. People sit and read the papers.

There might be a chess game going on; you never know who you'll be sat next to. Loads of people come and go. They might work here for a day or two or even a week. Some you never see them again – it could be a Pole at breakfast, a Frenchman at lunch and an Indian at supper – *they* make me feel like I've got as much right to be here as anyone else. I love it! I'm picking up so many new phrases in different languages. Anyway, there's never ever been a row like that.' Mary paused.

'What happened to the two women, then?' Robyn prompted.

'It was all over the park. People said it was the best bit of sauce they'd had in ages. But I didn't like it. There were fists and all, but then *he* stormed in,' Mary said.

'The Heron?' Robyn checked. 'Should have known he'd show up – he always does!'

'Yes, from nowhere,' Mary confirmed.

'He thinks he's the bee's knees,' Ned said.

'He does! How is he always where he needs to be? Go on.' Robyn waved a hand at Mary.

'And then he ranted at them about signing the Official Secrets Act. He told them off in front of us all. Said they'd disgraced themselves and the good name of Bletchley Park. Then he frogmarched them out of BP. I didn't see them after that. They were both off station in minutes.' Mary's eyes filled with tears. 'And no one has seen either of them since,' she added ominously.

'Is that what you and the Bow Tie were talking about, at the party?' she realised.

'Yes! It put the wind up us. They've disappeared into thin air,' Mary said with a shudder.

'Honestly, I told you both, didn't I? The Heron is far more dangerous than either of you realise,' Robyn said. 'So, what are we going to do about it?' she challenged them.

'Caves,' Ned said.

'Gallery,' Mary added.

'Island,' Robyn whispered, as the three of them sat listening to the wind outside, blowing across her garden.

'Of course! What an idiot. *Island!*' she shouted, jumping to her feet and laughing at Ned and Mary's confused faces. 'My island! No wonder they told me I wasn't allowed to go there any more. It's been staring us in the face this whole time.'

26

Robyn and Ned were searching for kindling in the woods. 'My father knows the comings and goings of every single vehicle,' she said. 'I could ask him a few questions, see what he knows. It might give us a clearer picture about who or what is coming in and out of the park.'

She spied a wintering grebe hovering at the edge of the lake, waiting for the water to thaw. A small muntjac, foraging in the ivy, was startled by the sound of their feet and dipped back into the woods, showing a scut the same colour as snow.

'Does he keep any records? My father keeps records of everything, down to the last nut and bolt. He's a right scrooge.'

'Yes! Well done, Ned. He writes it all down in his logbook. Just like Mr Samuels does for Joy and Charity.'

Being on an errand for her mother was a great excuse to find Ned and have a swift planning meeting.

'Is it in the house?' Ned asked, rubbing his hands together and blowing on them.

'No, he keeps it in the garages. All I have to do is get in

there undetected. I can see if there are any more vehicles in there as long as your father's hearse.'

'We,' Ned said, pulling his hat down over his ears.

'What?' Robyn raised her eyebrows, shoving the bits of broken branches into her basket.

'We, Robyn. All *we* have to do is get in there and find the notebook,' Ned said. 'It's us against them.'

Her father kept the keys to the garages on him at all times, clipped to his belt. She stroked the outline of her grandfather's penknife through the material of her dungarees. She barely wore any other outfit these days. Her mother had run her up another set. And she'd completely grown out of her school pinafore – not that she'd ever go back to wearing a dress now.

While Ned finished his jobs in the huts, Robyn dashed home, dumping the log basket by the range. She could hear her father scrubbing himself clean in the scullery, singing under his breath. Quickly she crept up to her parents' bedroom and lifted the keyring off his thick leather belt. Then she ran back down to the garages. It was getting dark, but Ned was there, although he'd have to tear back to the hearse before his father got there. Mary, who was now a proficient cyclist and had finished her deliveries in record time, was waiting with Ned.

'I've got just enough time to help search before I need to get back to Mrs Fisher's for a measly tea.' Mary grimaced.

'Let's make this fast, then,' Robyn said, unlocking the small door cut into the larger door. Using the torch, she found the logbook.

'Have a look and see if those words are there – *caves*, *gallery* and *island*,' Ned suggested.

'Do you think there might be caves under Bletchley Park?' Mary asked.

'Don't be daft. Who'd have had time to find caves, what with a war going on?' Ned gestured around him.

'Why not? It's got an island, so why not caves?' she said, turning the pages of the logbook.

'Exactly! My dad hears stories down the docks about tunnels and caves under Liverpool, round Edge Hill way,' Mary said with authority.

'That sounds like a tall tale. Like a story you tell kids about monsters and minotaurs.' Ned shook his head.

'Can you two stop blathering on about caves and help me read this list?' Robyn interrupted.

The three of them scanned the pages. There were lists of Army vehicles, Jeeps, trucks, private cars, the charabanc, ambulances, a decommissioned bus and other military transport. Robyn flicked through the pages, almost ripping one in her haste. Then she saw a word that looked Welsh.

'*Ogofâu?*' she read aloud.

'Is that German?' Ned asked.

'No, but it sounds close,' Mary said.

'It's Welsh, I think.' Robyn kept repeating it under her breath; it sounded so familiar.

'Can't you ask your mother? She's Welsh, isn't she?' Ned said.

'Yes, but won't it seem suspicious?' Mary wondered. 'That you're asking what random words mean?'

'I could weave it into the conversation, subtly?' Robyn offered, although subtlety was hardly her strong suit.

Once she spotted the word in her father's scrawl, she was

able to find it again. Then she saw two more words in what they decided had to be Welsh: *oriel* and *ynys*.

'You'd better get those keys back before they're missed,' Ned said, hearing the clock tower bells pealing. 'And we should all get home.'

Robyn put the keys back on her father's belt just in time. She heard him empty the tin bath out of the back door. Creeping out of her parents' bedroom, she felt triumphant until she saw her mother standing on the landing. Arms folded, face made from thunder and temper popping like lightning.

'What are you doing?' her mother asked.

'I . . . I was . . .'

She'd thought about getting caught and what she'd say. But she had worried about someone catching her in the garages, not at home.

'Well? I'm waiting.' Her mother stood blocking her exit. 'What were you doing with your father's keys?'

'I borrowed them.'

'What for? What do you want in the garages? Is that where you've been, then? I thought you were still in the loft with Mr Samuels.'

'I needed something.'

'From your father's garages?' her mother said in disbelief.

'A . . . tyre!' She remembered the tyre and the tree swing. 'I needed a tyre. I know I should have asked and I'm sorry, but I didn't think anyone would mind,' she said.

'Whatever for?'

'A swing.'

'I see. Well, you should have asked permission, Robyn.

You're not supposed to be in there any more. Remember?'

'Sorry,' she said, hanging her head. 'What does *ynys* mean?' she blurted out, desperate to change the subject.

'Ynys? You're interested in learning Welsh, are you?' Her mother perked up.

They'd been right. It *was* Welsh!

'I heard someone say it, in the cafeteria.' Robyn crossed her fingers behind her back.

There were loads of Welsh people at the park; she was on safe ground.

'It means island. Is that where you're building the swing? Because you can think again. You know you're not allowed on the island any more.' Her mother sighed.

But Robyn didn't care, because they were on to something. *Caves. Gallery. Island. Ogofâu. Oriel. Ynys.*

'What's going on?' her father said, coming up the stairs in his dressing gown, rubbing his hair dry with a small towel.

'This one – taking tyres to make swings on the *ynys* she's not allowed on any more.'

'I took your keys for the garages and borrowed a tyre to make a swing. I know it was stupid and I'm sorry,' she reeled off.

'Well,' her mother said, 'that Woolton pie won't bake itself, mind, and I've got orders for tomorrow.' Her mother's empire was expanding as swiftly as the park's staff: there were thousands of them now.

'Lot of trouble for a tyre. I'd have found you one if you'd only asked, Birdy. I know you're up to something. Whatever it is, stay out of the garages and off that island,' her father said, then closed the bedroom door softly.

27

February 1940

Frogspawn as thick as jelly bobbed beneath the surface of the lake. Jet-black eyes stared at Robyn from the solid mass of imperfect globes. Hungry, unblinking water-boatmen approached the unsuspecting spawn. Last year, before the war came, clumps of tadpoles had formed in the lake, but nothing ever came of them – maybe it was a warning of what was to come. The spawn, instead of flourishing, had failed and floated across the lake before thinning out into nothingness. She hoped that wouldn't happen again this year.

'So, what's the plan now?' Ned said, joining her on the landing stage.

They'd been watching and waiting for weeks now, for the Heron to make a false move. Or at least give something away. But he seemed to have gone to ground.

'The Heron is hiding something, or someone, on the island. Whenever he comes back from wherever he's lurking, he's going to get it, or them, out of the park, in your father's hearse. All we have to do is find out what's on the island and when he's planning to make it disappear.'

'Easy-peasy, then!' Ned rolled his eyes.

'Is anyone about? No early birds dashing into work in their pyjamas?' She grinned, pulling off the clothes that she'd thrown on over her swimming costume.

'This is not a time for joking about, Robyn. But yes, the coast is clear. Are you sure about this?' Ned asked. 'We shouldn't be drawing attention to ourselves. Besides, it's going to be Baltic in there. You'll catch your death,' he hissed, as she stepped into the crisp icy water. 'Swimming is so dangerous. I don't know why you –'

Robyn stifled a scream as the cold stole the air from her lungs.

'Hurry up. Just a quick look, all right,' Ned warned, squinting at the clock tower. 'And don't freeze or anything, because I'm not jumping in to save you.'

The sooner she started moving, the sooner this would be over. Robyn nodded, then dived underwater so as to make less noise.

She had never swum in the lake this early in the year and never would again. Her limbs sang with pain. *Mind over matter*, she told herself, opening her eyes. Brown bullheads barrelled along the bed of the lake. Perch swam through freshwater algae. And snails slithered at the bases of long-stalked pondweed. The surface of the water was flecked with midges, disturbed by a kingfisher spearing its prey.

185

Reaching the island, she pulled herself up onto the bank. She rubbed her arms and legs roughly before searching every bush and climbing every tree. She wasn't sure what she was looking for, but it all appeared to be as she'd left it: not a branch out of place. Disappointed, and with a sense of dread, Robyn forced herself back into the water. Ned was waiting on the landing stage with towels and blankets and a flask of something hot, thank goodness.

'It doesn't look like anyone's even been on the island.' She shivered as he wrapped her up.

She had to get dry and warm, otherwise she'd be back in bed and under house watch from her mother again. Ned turned his back while she tugged her clothes back on, squeezing the lake out of her hair. He handed her a cup of black tea, which she sipped gratefully. As they walked back up to the Mansion, a skein of geese swooped over their heads, making Ned duck.

'Any footprints?' Ned asked. 'No sign of anything suspicious at all?'

'No. Only mine,' she said regretfully as they reached the hearse.

Although she hated the very sight of the hearse, at least its presence meant Ned was somewhere at the park. But in a matter of months, he was to leave and never return. His father had warned him that their work at the park would end by the summer. The huts were almost complete and it was time to resume business back at their workshop. Sadly, coffins and funerals were in high demand.

'Did you find out why he needs all these planks?' She

gestured to the open doors and the pile of wood in the back of the hearse.

'Yes, and you're not going to like it. It's not what we thought. It has nothing to do with the Heron. One of the women received a box of flowers from her boyfriend. She kept the box to store those long message slips in, and that ticker tape roll they use for something. Anyway, we started making up racks of the boxes for the rest of the staff to store their printouts in.'

'Strange thing to store paperwork in, isn't it?' she said.

'There's nothing suspicious about it. Anyway, this one has the brickyard address on it. It must be more paperwork.' Ned pointed to a long box in the hearse; it had an address printed on it.

'Might be something exciting for your mother to process!' She couldn't think of a job duller than an admin role in a brickyard.

'We'll have to drop it off for her on the way home,' Ned said.

'Anyway, I'd better check on Joy's eggs.' Robyn nodded up at the loft. 'Mr Samuels showed me how to shine a torch through them to see the squab inside.'

'That's creepy.'

'It's life, Ned. Joy has made life. There's nothing creepy about that. She's a healthy pigeon, that's what they're supposed to do.'

Speaking of health, Mr Samuels had made it clear, ever since the bombing, that Robyn was only to come up to the loft if she was feeling well. It wasn't as if she had to clock in and out like the rest of the staff at Bletchley. Besides, since Joy had laid her eggs, there was nowhere else she'd rather be. She'd resigned herself to the fact that this apprenticeship might never lead to one in the garages. If her parents thought she was in the loft, they didn't plague her with questions about how she'd spent her day. And Mr Samuels never asked her where she'd been or when she'd be back. She was left to her own devices, which was a welcome novelty. She might not even go back to school once the war was over. She'd ask Mr Samuels if he could find her permanent work at the park, as she liked working with him and the birds.

'Have you decided what you'll call them, when they hatch?' Ned asked. Mr Samuels had given Robyn the honour of naming them, and hand-rearing them if they hatched while Joy was out on a mission.

'Dilly and Alice,' she said. 'Dilly is Mr Knox's name, he's called Dillwyn. I heard the Bow Tie call him it through the kitchen window. But Dillwyn's a bit of a mouthful for a baby bird.'

'He's Welsh?' Ned said gasping. '*Mr Knox* is Welsh? Caves. Gallery. Island!'

'Yes, *yes*! I know. It took me by surprise too because he doesn't have an accent like my mam, but I don't think he's guilty. The Heron's got it all wrong if he thinks Mr Knox is a spy.'

'The Heron's been reading too many Agatha Christies! Could it be your mother?' Ned joked. 'I've seen the stack of paperbacks from the library on your kitchen table.'

'Shut up, Ned! My mam's not a spy. She hasn't time to

read murder mysteries, let alone supply the writer with secrets! I'll see you later.' She dashed off.

There was only one name on the suspect list, as far as Robyn was concerned. She couldn't understand why the adults were blind to what was staring them in the face. They all seemed in awe of him – even Mr Knox, she thought, remembering the disrespectful way the Heron had spoken to him in the woods. She had been so sure about the island. But she wasn't giving up on proving them wrong about him yet. There were still *caves* and *gallery*, and that meant there was still hope.

28

March 1940

Today was the day. Mr Samuels had promised her she could wait for Joy to land and take the capsule from her. Joy, Charity, Faith and Hope should be returning from a covert mission to an unnamed destination. Robyn had gleaned this much from studiously listening to Mr Samuels on the telephone. Since her failure to find anything incriminating on the island, she had started making notes in a pocketbook Mr Samuels had given her. Admittedly there wasn't much in it yet, apart from her sketches, but all the same, she kept it hidden in her overalls. She'd also taken to keeping a stubby pencil tucked behind her ear, in case she needed it. Robyn still had no idea where the agent would take the birds: France or Germany. All she knew was the carriers were to collect coded messages and bring them back to Bletchley and Sandringham and maybe Windsor too. Whenever Joy came back, the bird was all hers. That much had been firmly agreed.

Robyn was desperate for Joy to meet her squabs, Dilly and Alice, who had hatched while their mother was away on her mission. She was a little worried about how Joy would react when she saw Alice's foot. She hoped Joy wouldn't reject her. Alice's differences were what made her interesting and unique, and Robyn couldn't help but love her even more for it. Mr Samuels said the yellow and pink warts on Alice's foot were a form of pigeonpox. Robyn had her own scars from chickenpox so she liked to think that she knew how Alice felt, although she doubted the other pigeons would chase her around the loft and call her *Leper Lewis* as some of the children had done in the playground to Robyn. Dilly and Alice would be out there soon enough, flying high.

Mr Samuels was making the rounds. He noted down changes in the pigeons' behaviour, their condition and bowel movements. Robyn cleaned out the hutches, replaced the water and fed those who Mr Samuels hadn't already fed. She had to keep her mind on the job. Everything would be better once Joy returned.

'I'm away to fetch some more water for the girls, lass. Keep a close watch, now,' Mr Samuels said.

As if she needed telling, Robyn thought, but nodded all the same. She heard the door to the loft click back open in the draft – all the windows were open. Robyn was ready to close the door when she heard *his* voice – the Heron – coming from the gallery. She peered out cautiously, but couldn't see him. Where was his voice coming from? There was nowhere else to go up here other than the loft and the gallery. Perhaps he was coming up the stairs?

She held her breath as she peered through the gap in the door. She could hear the Heron talking to someone but she still couldn't see him. Then she gasped as an enormous oil painting on the wall opposite swung outwards and from behind it appeared the Heron! He was soon followed by another man.

'So, Doves in the hearse but the rest in the brickyard via the freight trains,' the Heron finished.

Doves! *Codename: Doves*!

'Castles . . . Scattered across Wales was always a lottery,' the other man agreed. 'Especially with alcohol involved. He was in no fit state to care for himself, let alone . . .'

'Indeed. The trap is set. And now we wait,' the Heron said.

As the men began to descend the stairs, their heavy footfalls masked their words. Why were they moving doves on freight trains? Did they mean the carrier pigeons? Robyn inched the door open. The long painting was motionless now. As if nothing unusual had happened. She looked around before reaching out to touch it. Robyn listened to hear the men returning, but they didn't. She waited, then pushed the painting a little more firmly, but nothing happened. She walked backwards along the gallery, looking at the painting and its position on the wall. There wasn't anywhere higher than the loft – so where had the men come from? She was certain they wouldn't have just stood behind the painting to hold a conversation. They must have a secret room somewhere.

Gallery! *Island* had been wrong but that didn't mean that *caves* and *gallery* were wrong too. The man at her parents' party – Mr Turing – he'd been certain about *gallery* and *caves*, but less so about *island*. And he'd been talking to a Welshman! Could he have something to do with it? There were so many possibilities, it was making her head spin. She needed to think, and she could only do that outside. Robyn ran down the stairs, through the wood-panelled hall and out to the front of the Mansion. She closed her eyes and tried to picture the inside: the loft, the staircase, and their positions. She ran around the perimeter of the building, looking up at all the windows, and then she saw it: the green dome. Were there caves underneath the Mansion, and did the dome hide the entrance?

There was only one way to find out. She had to make that picture move.

29

Mr Samuels burst through the loft door as the bell rang. They rushed over to the platform. Joy was on it, but she wasn't standing. She was lying down, covered in a tar-like substance that smelt like Robyn's father's garage. Mr Samuels picked the pigeon up, cradling her in his big hands.

'*Oh no!* My lady,' he said in alarm.

Adults don't panic, Robyn thought. *They always know what to do.* But Mr Samuels stood and stared at Joy as if he didn't know where to start. She smelt of the sea and her feathers were crusty-looking.

'What's happened to her?' Robyn asked, hoping to shock Mr Samuels into some kind of action but for a few painful seconds he just stood there, as if he hadn't even heard what she'd said.

Finally, he started to move. Running with Joy to the bureau, Mr Samuels set her down on a towel and rummaged in his kit bag, pulling out a first-aid tin.

'Here, clean her with this. Carefully.' He passed Robyn a

cloth and a small bottle of iodine. 'We need to get that oil off her feathers before it mats and gives her hypothermia.'

Mr Samuels was busy threading a needle and setting out scissors and tweezers. Robyn watched him fill a syringe from another bottle of clear liquid.

'For the pain. Smells like the seawater's got to her skin,' he explained. 'Clean her up,' he reminded.

Robyn opened her bottle and blotted some of the fluid onto the cloth. She wiped down Joy's slick feathers.

'There, there,' she said. 'We'll take care of all this, Joy, don't you worry.'

'That's it, well done, lass. Keep talking to her,' Mr Samuels said approvingly. He sounded more certain now. Perhaps he felt better when he was doing something too.

Robyn wiped the pigeon from top to bottom, turning the cloth. Each time it came away stained by the oil. She told Joy all about Dilly and Alice, trying to fill the awful silence in the loft. As Joy's feathers eventually lightened, she saw a different colour under the black: red.

'Joy's bleeding!' she said in alarm.

Mr Samuels moved her to one side and took a closer look at Joy's wing.

'You're right: it must have been a hawk. He's made a dead set at her. Got her here, see?' He moved so she could see the wound better. 'Talons in and ripped a hole, but it's old. It's dried blood.'

'Is that good or bad?'

'Depends on the damage. Give me that.' He gestured for the cloth. 'Need to get all this oil off and see how bad it is. Run down and boil a kettle for the hot water bottle. We need to warm her up.'

Downstairs was the last place Robyn wanted to go. She didn't need to run into the Heron, especially not after what she'd seen and heard on the gallery, but watching Joy's ribcage rise and fall pitifully, there was no choice. She'd have to be careful and quick and hope that he didn't see her.

As Robyn returned the kettle to the makeshift kitchenette next to the ballroom, she spotted Mary going into the library. Robyn followed her, looking around for a librarian but the room was empty.

'Mary!' she said quietly, beckoning her friend to the far corner of the library, away from the door and passers-by.

'What are you doing in here?' Mary whispered. 'You can't be in here while I do the pinches.' Mary moved some sheets of paper out of sight.

'What are pinches? And why are you doing them? Never mind, there isn't time. We need to meet, the three of us, I've got something to tell you. You won't believe it . . . Wait, why aren't you delivering messages for Mr Knox?'

'He's not here,' Mary said, finally getting a word in.

'What do you mean, he's not here? Mr Knox is always here.'

'He's gone, Robyn. He's left Bletchley!' Mary looked distraught.

'What? When?'

'I went to the cottage to deliver the books he ordered but he wasn't there. One of the ladies put the books on his desk and asked me to join them for a cup of sweet tea, for the shock . . .' Mary hesitated.

'What did they say, Mary?'

'The Bow Tie said Mr Knox had gone home to Courns Wood, which must be his house, to recover. The other woman, the one with the wavy hair, Mavis or Margaret, was quite cross. It was because of the Heron, but they wouldn't tell me anything much. The Bow Tie said she they didn't know when he'd be back. Something about when he got his orders from above,' Mary clarified.

'We've got to do something! We can't let them accuse Mr Knox of being a spy when we know it's the Heron. Believe me when I tell you I absolutely know it is him. Oh, I need to talk to you, Mary, but I've got to stay in the loft with Joy.' She stopped talking, because if she carried on she would lose control of herself.

'Why? What's happened?' Mary asked.

'A hawk attacked her. She's covered in oil.'

'*Oh no!* I'm so sorry. Is she . . . will she be all right?' Mary asked.

'I don't know. I have to go.' Then she said recklessly, 'But there's good news too. I know how to prove the Heron is the traitor and not Mr Knox.'

30

May 1940

From the kitchen window Robyn watched a speckle-bellied song thrush select the tallest tree. Staging herself on the highest branch, the thrush performed a solo.

Robin would far rather tune in to the bird than to the wireless right now. There was only so much space in her head for all the information it was currently holding. Her parents listened to the radio morning and night, trying to make head or tail of the coded messages the broadcasters read out. 'The woman stroked the dog's nose' seemed so ridiculous it had made her laugh, which resulted in a thorough talking-to. Apparently it would, according to her parents, 'make sense to someone somewhere out in the field' and 'could save lives' and was 'no laughing matter'.

Nothing was a laughing matter to them any more. Mr

Churchill, the new prime minister, had just announced, 'I have nothing to offer but blood, toil, tears and sweat.' Her parents stood up and clapped at that. Robyn found their display embarrassing. She had gone as far as nodding her head in agreement with Mr Churchill. Everything had changed since the shocking retreat at Dunkirk. The occupation of France was a bleak warning to them all. No one could say with any certainty, 'They won't invade us!' Mr Chamberlain was no longer in charge of their country. He'd seemed so hopeful after the peace treaty in Munich. Everyone had been.

'Churchill's the right man for the job,' her father said to her mother. 'He'll see us through. Won't get taken for a fool or trust a word the enemy says – that's not worth the paper it's written on, what a waste of time. And make no mistake, Churchill doesn't hope to keep the enemy at bay with smiles and handshakes. He means to win the damned war!'

Robyn thought about all the other people listening in from their homes. Soldiers fighting, nurses, ambulance drivers, workers in munitions factories, sailors on ships and members of the RAF flying across the world, all listening to the same words. She was connected to each of them, through Mr Churchill's words. They were all hearing them at the exact same time, vowing never to give in, never to surrender.

Sounds like high-pitched accordion notes came from lapwings. It started to rain as she watched them somersault through the sky, showing off their white undercarriages, and wondered when Joy would fly again. For the last month Robyn had spent every second she could at Joy's side, looking after her and her squabs. She'd had to reluctantly abandon her plans to work out how the Heron made the painting move. As Ned had said, when she told him and Mary what she'd seen, it wasn't as if the painting was going anywhere. She was relieved they'd both understood that Joy came first. Robyn knew in her heart that although Dilly and Alice were thriving, Joy was not. Joy had brought back an important message, but no message could be worth the wounds she had sustained.

'Never was so much owed by so many to so few,' Mr Churchill finished as her father switched off the wireless.

The three of them sat for a moment in the kitchen and didn't speak as the rain and wind lashed at the windowpanes.

'At least that'll slow things down tonight,' her father said as he finished his tea.

'Might be a storm too.' Her mother nodded towards the window. 'Let's hope it brings some winds of change. We could all do with some good luck, couldn't we?'

'Speaking of change, I've got some news,' her father said, putting down his cigarette tin. 'Mr Knox isn't coming back. I'm only telling you because Mr D has said I can. An announcement will be made to all staff tomorrow. There'll be some movement next door and I'm not sure if the ladies will still work in there or –'

'What do you mean – not coming back? What, not ever?' Robyn turned from the window where she'd been watching the drops of rain chase one another down the pane.

'Seems that way,' he said, pouring another cup of tea.

Her mother was unusually quiet on the matter, her face poker straight. 'I always liked him,' she finally said. She swept the crumbs off the table into her hand and threw them into the chicken bucket. '*Shame.* You think you know people, and then they . . .' she tailed off.

'What's a shame?' Robyn asked, but neither of her parents would answer or even look at her. 'Why isn't Mr Knox coming back? I bet it's to do with –' She stopped herself just before she said *the Heron.*

'Might be lightning too.' Her father changed the subject, spooning in another sugar.

'What's a shame about Mr Knox?' Robyn tried again. 'What's he done? What's he been accused of?' she dared.

'Nothing to worry yourself about,' her mother said.

'Fine. Then I'm going out,' she announced.

'In this weather?' Her father raised his eyes from his newspaper.

'Where?' her mother asked.

'To the loft. There's something I forgot to do,' she lied.

Seizing the moment, she grabbed her wellingtons. The news about Mr Knox changed everything! She couldn't leave it any longer. She had to find out what was behind that painting and clear Mr Knox's name – tonight, before it was too late. Her gut told her that behind the painting there had to be some kind of stairway down to a cave. If the code words were right, *gallery* and *caves* must be connected. *Island* must have been a mistake, she decided as she reached the door to the loft.

'DAMN IT!' she heard Mr Samuels shout from inside the loft.

Robyn opened the door. He was holding the telephone receiver in his hand, staring into space. She held her damp mac out in front of her. The smell reminded her of her gas mask, which she was told she should carry about with her.

'Are you all right? Excuse me, Mr Samuels? I said, are you all right?' she repeated, walking across to him, her mac dripping on the floorboards.

Her words made him jump. He dropped the receiver, which clanked against the wood of the bureau.

'The enemy have issued an ordinance stating that all carrier pigeons are to be killed. They've trained hawks, as falcons weren't working. Hawks loop low over the ground, see, and can stalk their prey for miles. They're fleet and fierce. And hawks are always hungry and ready to hunt.'

'What? They can't! Why would they do that?' Robyn was appalled.

'When our agents parachute in behind enemy lines, our birds – often Joy, Charity, Hope and Faith – are with them. As you know, the pigeons then carry coded intel back to us here, which we relay to Mr Churchill, and London, for further action. And they're doing a top job – that's the trouble, Robyn. Our winged messengers are a menace to the enemy.'

'How could Joy be a menace?' She would fight anyone who tried to harm a feather on Joy's head.

'Because the intel they're carrying back is vital to Allied operations. These birds have uncovered more information about secret weapons the enemy are going to use against us, than you and I have had hot dinners.'

'But they're animals, not soldiers. Joy didn't join up!' Robyn protested. 'She doesn't deserve to die!'

'This isn't a game. It's a war, Robyn. People will do all kinds of things you never thought possible.' He placed the receiver back on the cradle. 'Even to animals.'

'They're going to attack our birds and try and kill them? Is that what happened to Joy?' she asked in disbelief. If the pigeons weren't safe and able to do their job, none of them were.

'Happen it was, lass. The only real constant in the natural world is change. Us folk have to find a way to keep up,' Mr Samuels said.

Robyn opened the door to Joy's hutch, held out her hand and felt the rush of warmth and affection as she stroked Joy's skull.

'She's not getting better, is she?' This was what she should be concentrating on: Joy, her lady, not the Heron.

'Don't miss a trick, do you, lass?' Mr Samuels said. 'Aye, Joy's looking a tad time-ridden.'

Since the night the bombs fell on Bletchley, she'd known that Joy not only tolerated her but liked and trusted her. She made sure to do her duty by the other pigeons; she fed and watered them, as well as cleaning out their hutches. But when she looked in Joy's eyes, there was a connection. And Joy didn't look away any more. Instead, she returned Robyn's gaze, and they had whole conversations without words.

'I'll take good care of her,' he said. 'I'll stay with her the night. I'll not leave her side. It's late and your mam and dad will be wondering where you've got to. You've spent enough time up here these past few weeks. Lass, you've done everything you could.'

'All right, then.' Robyn put on her dripping wet mac and squelched across the floor, the sound masking her sobs.

31

July 1940

The weather had been cloudless for the past three days, so the people of Bletchley could watch the dogfights in the sky as the enemy relentlessly attacked. But today the quiet was startling after the menacing racket of enemy planes taking on the RAF's Hurricanes and Spitfires, battling for not just Britain but for all of Europe. They'd be back though. Even if they'd retreated for now, the quiet wouldn't last. A lone peregrine falcon scaled the blue, luxuriating in the unexpected peace, and it was hard for Robyn to say where the sky ended and the lake began. The curved bill of a curlew climbed with heroic effort before fluting its descent. She listened as it repeated the pattern, like the chorus to a familiar song.

Mary finally got her breath back and began to speak in

gasps. 'I've made a mistake. A really terrible mistake and I've ruined everything – all our plans. I'm so sorry, Robyn.'

'Hang on, start at the beginning.' Robyn put both hands on Mary's shoulders. Her friend was shaking.

'I was waiting outside Mr Knox's cottage, for one of the ladies to answer the door –'

'Are they still working, then? Without him?' Ned interrupted, picking up Mary's bicycle to lean it against the landing stage.

'They're managing fine without him, from what I can see,' Robyn said admiringly. 'Besides, they can hardly take a break. Not now. Go on, Mary,' she instructed.

'They were talking about creating a system or a code and I couldn't stop myself. When they let me in, I blurted out my suggestion and –'

'What did you say? Things are already bad enough.'

'They needed a new way to send and receive coded telegrams. Like the ones I deliver to and from agents. I had my *Alice* book in my bag and said that they could use it. One of the ladies has her own copy, see?'

'I don't get it. What's wrong with that?' Ned asked.

'The agent and the coder both have the same book and an empty notebook filled with the same numbers in sets of five. They've made their own code.'

'I still don't understand,' Ned asked. 'How does it work?'

Robyn looked around, checking to make sure they were alone. The lake was still and empty, apart from the tadpoles, which had now changed into frogs, their slick legs stretching out behind them. No adults were up and walking around it, or cycling to the newly built huts. She suspected the park was almost full to bursting.

'Me and our Sybil used to play this game when Dad took us to the library. We'd choose copies of the same book. I'd pick out a word on a page and write down three numbers: the page, the line and how many words across it was. Sybil, using her copy, would work out what my message was. Simple. The ladies got excited. They must have . . .' Mary's voice cracked.

'Mentioned it to someone who told the Heron?' Ned guessed.

'No! They never would,' Robyn protested.

'How could I have been so stupid? I should never have shown off like that,' Mary sighed.

'I'm sure you weren't showing off, Mary,' Ned said kindly.

'It's not an offence, is it? It doesn't make you a fifth columnist or a spy,' said Robyn.

'And you haven't broken the Official Secrets Act,' Ned said, putting his arm around Mary.

'Your *Alice in Wonderland* code idea has nothing to do with *Codename: Doves*,' Robyn reminded her.

'Or caves, galleries or islands!' Ned added.

'But the Heron wants to interview me in the Mansion!' Mary's voice shook.

'Oh no! That's all we need!' Ned said before he could stop himself.

'He's probably interviewing everyone though. He'll have a long list to work through before he gets to you.' Robyn tried to sound reassuring. 'It could be ages away. Weeks or months even.'

'And I know he'll say it's because I'm a known contact of Mr Knox's. But it's not going to be about that any more, is it? It's so much worse! Why was I such a go-ahead girl about my great big idea?' Mary put her head in her hands.

'Because you're clever and you're the sort of person we need around here. Someone with big ideas. This place is chock-full of them,' Robyn said, thinking about Alan – the Prof.

'But look where it's got me. I'm dreading going into his study. I don't know what he's going to ask me or what I should say. I don't want to be on my own with him.'

'But this is perfect!' Robyn exclaimed, delighted. 'This is absolutely perfect, Mary! Don't you see? While the Heron is acting like the lord of the manor, Ned and I can sneak up to the gallery and find out how to make that painting open. Things are finally falling into place thanks to your mistake, Mary. Now all we have to do is wait for him to summon you.'

'Oh. Great,' Mary said, sounding defeated. 'Something to look forward to!'

'I wish we could come in with you,' Robyn offered, hoping that she sounded like she meant it.

'We honestly would if we could,' Ned added. Robyn could see he was just as excited as she was.

An uncomfortable silence fell over the three of them. Robyn looked around. She was searching for something comforting to say to Mary, who was going to have the worst part in her new plan, but she was distracted by a heron. It left its post on an oak tree, dropping to the lake with the grace of a dancer. It seized a duckling in one fell swoop and landed on the bank opposite them. The heron swallowed the duckling whole before Robyn could process what was happening. A mother duck quacked and clamoured in the rushes, trying to hide her other babies.

'No! Get away, you beast! Leave them alone!' Robyn screamed, jumping up and running at the heron. But the heron leapt into the sky, belly full, and flew off without a second thought for the tragedy it left behind.

32

September 1940

'Liverpool got it heavy last night, my mum said. Lots of the ports and dockyards did. Does Mary know?' Ned asked as they entered the Mansion.

'She's in with the Heron now. I haven't seen her yet. I suppose she knows,' Robyn said. 'Shall we go, then?'

They made their way up to the gallery.

'The man on the wireless described it like a torch ablaze,' Ned said.

'They said you could see it from a hundred miles away,' Robyn replied, keeping pace with him.

'My father said we weren't to look; said we shouldn't be spectators of someone else's tragedy. He says we see enough of that in the parlour where we're witness to enough misery.'

'He's a cheery one, isn't he? Great at keeping up morale.

Anyway, I thought it was London having it hot, not people up North,' Robyn said as they reached the gallery. 'They say the airborne fighting is over and the enemy plans to throw everything they've got at London.'

'Who knows what their plans are? All I know is that hundreds of people were killed,' Ned said sadly. 'We just have to hope that Mary's family are alive.'

'It's awful, isn't it? Can't imagine that amount of people just . . . *gone*!' She stopped, seeing Ned's face. 'What do you think happens, after?'

'You're asking me? The undertaker's boy who lives in a funeral parlour? Nothing. I think when you die, you're gone. I hate this, not knowing where Rob and Joe are . . . or if they're coming home . . .' he broke off.

'I don't know what to say, Ned. It must be dreadful,' Robyn said, putting a hand on his arm.

'My mother said the king is going to visit.' Ned changed the subject. 'She loves the Royal Family. Follows their every step.'

'I thought it was just a rumour that the king's coming here?'

'No. I meant Liverpool and the East End. Although I did hear some gossip in the huts that the king has already been here!'

'And we missed it? Surely not!' Robyn protested. 'Where'd you hear that?'

'Just some of the men in the huts talking. This place is bursting at the seams with secrets.'

'That's true,' Robyn agreed. 'Do you think he'll bring the princesses with him if he comes again?'

210

'Course not! It's dangerous enough him turning up here – just think of the fuss and bother if anyone saw him.'

'S'pose. Wonder why he did come? Probably to see Mr D. I guess we'll never know.

My mam's got a picture of the king on the kitchen wall. I'd have never heard the end of it if she'd met him. She says the queen's started a sewing bee at Buckingham Palace.'

'What good's a sewing bee if you're bombed out of your house?' Ned said angrily, as they hovered by the painting.

'I don't know, Ned, but it's kind of her all the same, isn't it?' Robyn wondered if they were going to have an argument.

'I mean, it's not like they're in it with the rest of us, are they?'

'Um, yes, they are. They were bombed too, you know. They could have left, fled to Canada,' she reasoned. 'The queen said the king will never leave Britain, and she'll never leave the king, and the princesses will never leave her. I thought that was very brave of her.'

'They're hardly roughing it with the rest of us, though, are they? Living the high life in their castles and palaces with servants, thrones, crowns and jewels. And they've got guards to keep them safe and all kinds. No Germans are going to invade their home, are they?'

'Well, I don't know.' She paused, thinking about her father and Mr Samuels and their strange visit to Sandringham. 'But I'm sure they're on rations, same as us. And Buck Palace was bombed too, just like here. BP and BP!' She smiled.

'Look, are we going to go through this painting or not? My father won't be long and we definitely do not want him

211

on the warpath.' Ned shuddered. 'He's gone to hand in his pass and sign out with security, before we drop off some packages at the brickyard,' Ned continued, looking at the painting in front of them, rather than at her.

She could tell he was on edge. Everyone was. Robyn bit her tongue, realising that nothing she could say would make things better for him, so instead she reached for his hand and squeezed it. She followed Ned's eyes, which were drawn to the flag of Great Britain and the brightly coloured bunting in the top right corner of the painting. In contrast, the serious men in their hats and suits looked like the Heron – she could see why he'd chosen it. It reminded her of the painting in his study, the Lowry he'd shown off about. All the children in this picture were pushed to the back, hovering at the edges of the world, like they did here at the park.

'This is our best chance to find out what's going on.' She gestured at the painting.

It wasn't just their best chance. It might be their only chance, because Ned's time at the park was ending. She'd almost forgotten that he lived elsewhere and had another life outside of Bletchley, and she wasn't ready to imagine life without Ned. So she didn't want to end things on a cross note. Ned and Mary were her only friends. If the Heron suspected Mary of anything, he might send her away, like Mr Knox, and then she'd really be on her own.

'Well, it's been nice knowing you, Miss Robyn Audrey Lewis,' Ned said.

He held his hand out. She wondered if it was a peace offering as well as a goodbye.

'You too, Master Ned Ian Letton.' She shook his hand enthusiastically.

'Do you remember that first day?' Ned said.

'Of course. How it all began.' She bit her lip.

'You and that bucket of poo by the hearse.' Ned grinned.

'Don't!' She couldn't believe it was over.

'I thought you were so strange!' he admitted.

'Oi! I thought the same about you. How will Mary and I manage without you, Ned?'

'You'll get by,' he joked.

'So, this could be it,' she said.

'The very last thing we do together,' he agreed.

'And it could be the stupidest,' she laughed.

'The daftest,' he said.

'The most dangerous,' she added.

'But that's not going to stop us, is it?' he checked.

'Not on your life,' she confirmed.

They both reached out to the painting, checking each corner. They ran their hands over the frame and their fingertips behind it. They stood back and looked at it. How had the Heron made it move? It seemed impossible. With her finger Robyn drew a line in the air dividing the painting in two and gestured to Ned to take one side. Inching along, they analysed every brush stroke, not wanting to miss a thing.

A loud creak from behind the painting jolted them. Wordlessly, they removed their hands from the frame and raced over to the loft. They hid behind the door, both trying hard not to breathe too loudly. Robyn knelt down to look through the keyhole, not daring to open the door.

The great, tall painting began to swing forward. Behind it was the top of a ladder. From somewhere inside a foot emerged, resting on the top rung. It wore a dark grey shoe, shiny and spotless.

When the Heron stepped out, Robyn put her hand over her mouth. Ned's eyes widened fit to burst, which was enormously satisfying. It was true. *Here* was the proof. This was happening right in front of them; if only Mary were here too, it would be perfect.

Robyn watched the Heron soundlessly climb down from the painting and out onto the gallery. When he pushed the painting back with his gloved hands there came a magnetic click and release of air, like a sigh. That must be why he always wore the brown leather gloves, there must be a mechanism inside the fingertips. Was it a key, a catch or even a magnet? Would a normal magnet work? There must be one in her father's garage, although she'd promised to keep out of there.

'*Caves*,' Ned mouthed, all awkwardness between them gone.

'*Gallery*,' Robyn confirmed, grinning wildly at him.

All they needed to figure out now was where the ladder led to and, more importantly, why the Heron went down there.

33

From the loft, Robyn watched the adults swarming like ants, marching from their huts to the Mansion and from the Mansion to the canteen.

'Why did the Heron get in Ned's hearse?' Mary said in dismay.

'I don't know. He's been obsessed with that hearse from the beginning,' Robyn replied.

'Did he say something about doves and freight trains?' Mary asked.

'Yes, so?'

'Doesn't a train stop in the brickyard where Ned's mum works?'

'Yes!' Robyn exclaimed, turning away from the window as the hearse rolled out of the big gates and headed towards the town. 'It's along the train line.'

'Could they be putting the carrier pigeons on trains?' Mary wondered.

'Why the brickyard? That's got nothing to do with

Bletchley and codes and spies, has it?' Robyn said.

'Or doves or pigeons, come to that!' Mary agreed.

'What if he's passing on information about *Codename: Doves*?' Robyn didn't want to link Joy and the pigeons to the Heron in any way, but what else could *doves* mean, here at Bletchley Park?

'We're going to have to wait until Ned finds a way of reporting back to us. If he can,' Mary said.

'I hate the thought of him trapped in that hideous hearse, with that dreadful man!' Robyn almost spat in disgust.

'If only we could get that painting to open, we could find out where the Heron popped up from,' Mary said.

'We did everything he did, except we need those gloves. It's impossible, Mary. I'm tempted to smash it up,' she said recklessly. 'I'd like to rip a big hole in it and –'

'Where do you think the ladder leads to?' Mary interrupted.

'It must be a tunnel down to a cave. I bet there's a basement in here that we don't know about,' Robyn said. 'We can add it to the extensive list of things we don't know about!'

'There are rumours at the park about a tunnel. They say it leads to the train station. But why would the Heron be using it? He could walk out of here and get the train! Unless he's a smuggler,' Mary said.

'Don't be daft! He didn't have anything with him. Besides, what would he smuggle in and out of the park through a tunnel? All I've seen him with, at the park, are Mr Knox's files, and he hardly needs a tunnel to sneak those out.' Robyn rolled her eyes.

'Especially as now he's got rid of Mr Knox he can intercept

all the post and messages he likes,' Mary added, frowning. 'Should we tell someone?'

'If we tell the adults about all this –' Robyn waved her hand around – 'they'll never believe us. They'll say it was all in our heads or that we have overactive imaginations.'

'But you and Ned saw the Heron climb out of a painting!' Mary reasoned.

'They'd never believe me, not with my track record. And Ned's gone, hasn't he? Who knows when we'll be able to see him again now his father's finished working here? They're not going to let him back into the park on his own, are they?'

'They've put even more guards on the gates. What do you think is going on? It feels like something is happening, doesn't it? Like there's a change coming. I can feel it.' Mary looked worried. 'And I don't just mean the blitz in London, I mean something here.'

'Tell me what the Heron said when he interviewed you?' Robyn asked.

'*Again?*' Mary sighed before continuing. 'Hundreds of questions about Mr Knox and the cottages. What kind of work went on in there. And what kind of conversations did the ladies have. He wanted to know what sort of messages I deliver. Then what I'd seen about the park in the huts and all that,' Mary repeated.

'And what about the children's book code you told the ladies about?' Robyn prompted.

'I told them about the game me and our Sybil played, and that was it. He lost interest then because somebody else turned up at the door.' Mary smiled.

217

'Who? You didn't say that part before.' Robyn turned away from the window.

'Three officers. American from the way they were dressed. So glamorous! Looked like they'd hopped right out of Hollywood,' she said admiringly. 'I'd like to hop right out of this place and go home,' she added.

But Mary no longer had a home to hop to. Mary's family were on the council waiting list to be rehoused. Mary's father had forbidden her to return to Liverpool. He wrote that she'd be safer if she stayed in the town of Bletchley. *If only he knew!*

'I want to go home, Robyn.'

'I know, but you're safe while you're still here. I'm worried he might send you away.'

'I'm useless here, far away from my family. I'm not sure how much longer I can stick it, to be honest with you.' Mary sighed.

'That's another thing: what are the Americans doing over here, far from *their* home? Don't you think it's a bit fishy? Did you see any files on his desk? Anything with doves on?' she asked hopefully, passing Dilly and Alice clean water bowls.

'No. His desk was completely clear. All shipshape,' Mary said.

'It was covered in files and paperwork when I went in. You don't think he's leaving? Is that why he's gone with Ned's father? Are they in on it, do you think?'

'No! Ned's father can't be a spy. D'you reckon he's taking the Heron somewhere?' Mary said.

'How are we supposed to stop the Heron from running away with . . . *state secrets*? Can't you sneak into his office? I'd go, but I don't want to take my eyes off that painting, or Joy,' Robyn explained. 'Can't you pretend you have something to deliver? A message to put on his desk?'

'No way! What would I say to his secretary? Miss Hughes would take the message from me, wouldn't she? She's not going to let *me* waltz into his office! Anyway, I've got to go. The Bow Tie's got me on another special job in the library,' Mary said proudly. 'She caught me coming out of the Heron's office and saw how upset I was. I don't think the ladies in the cottage like the Heron, not after the way he treated Mr Knox. She said cataloguing in the library will take my mind off everything.'

When Mary returned to the library, Robyn went back up to the loft and passed the time by giving the hutches a good going-over – her mother would approve. Her parents had been easy to persuade when she'd broached the subject of sleeping in the loft to watch over Joy. When she'd passed her apprenticeship, her mother had handed her some lemon bonbons in a small paper bag. Her father gave her a pat on the shoulder and said they were both very proud of her. And, surprisingly, that had felt better than any certificate signed by Mrs Ashman from school.

Robyn leant back against Joy's hutch and hummed to her, even though the pigeon was already asleep.

'Her days as a carrier pigeon are over,' Mr Samuels had said, before setting off on another operation. Joy should be in retirement somewhere quiet and less dangerous. With Mr Samuels off site with Charity, Hope and Faith, and the Heron in the hearse, Robyn relaxed for the first time in months and let the sound of Joy's steady snores soothe her as she carried out her chores.

34

'I met Ned in the woods,' Mary said, panting. 'Well, I didn't meet him. He ambushed me – he was up a tree and jumped down. Scared the life out of me!' They'd run into the maze to meet after Mary had dropped off the post for Mr Samuels in the loft. Everywhere else was far too hectic, with people grabbing lunch from the canteen or coffees from her mother's hut. They couldn't risk being overheard.

'How did Ned get into the woods? Did he really make it past security?' Robyn was impressed. There were now extra guards on the front gates, a new sentry hut added and a further patrol at both side gates. Everyone had to show their pass and say their name and purpose. Mary was right: something was happening.

'He went down the spinney, shimmied over a fence and climbed up a tree in someone's back garden and came over that way. Through the air! In the trees – like Tarzan!' Mary was delighted.

'Blimey! And? What did he say?'

'They drove straight to the brickyard, as we suspected. Ned said the Heron practically jumped out of the hearse, before it had even stopped. And then he went to speak to Ned's mother!'

'Oh no!' she said in shock. 'Not her too?'

'Yes. Ned was horrified. The Heron, friends with both your parents! Or worse, they're in league with him!' Mary scrunched up her nose.

'Did Ned hear what they said?' she asked.

'No, his father turned the radio on!' Mary shook her head. 'He says his father never turns it on as it's disrespectful to the dead.'

She groaned. 'And then what happened?'

'The Heron beckoned Ned's father and he went into the brickyard too. When Ned's father came back out, a few minutes later, he made Ned walk home.'

'*What?* Why? He left his hearse at the brickyard. With the Heron?'

'Yes!' Mary shook her head in disbelief. 'I thought he was married to that thing!'

'Did Ned get a chance to see if anything was in the hearse?' Robyn shrugged off the image of a dead body. 'Was there anyone, or any*thing*, in the back?'

'He doesn't know. Says his father marched him home and then went into the showroom to quote for a coffin. But then Ned got on his bike and rode back to the brickyard.' Mary grinned.

'And?' Robyn's heart was thundering in her chest. 'Is he all right? What happened?'

'When he got to the brickyard, the Heron had disappeared. Vanished! Into thin air.' Mary clicked her fingers like a magician. 'And Ned said his mother was standing on her own, in front of a massive kiln shed, with a tape measure in her hand. She wrote something down in a notebook and then went to the hearse and did the same!'

'No! What was she measuring?'

'I don't know. And then . . .' Mary paused, 'she went back inside. Telephoned someone and Ned heard her say . . .' Mary waited for Robyn to fill in the gap.

'Doves?' She guessed, breathless with anticipation.

'*Doves!*' Mary clapped her hands. 'And . . . caves!'

'No! What about islands? Any mention?'

'He doesn't think so.'

'We've got something to go on, at last! Even without islands.'

'There's got to be a connection between the park and the brickyard. That's how the Heron got back here so fast,' Mary said.

'What do you mean, got back here?' Robyn asked, looking over her shoulder, even though they were quite hidden from sight, in the middle of the maze.

'Ned worked out roughly what time the Heron disappeared. When I was in the library, he came down the stairs – not that long after Ned had seen him at the brickyard. He talked to Miss Hughes for a bit then went into his office,' Mary said excitedly.

'Well, that explains things, a bit, sort of.' Robyn nodded.

'So why would the Heron want to sneak from the park to the brickyard, unseen?' Mary wondered.

'And what's Ned's mum measuring?' Robyn asked.

'And more importantly, exactly what is in the back of that hearse?' Mary added. 'Any bright ideas, Robyn?'

'Well, I might have one or two up my sleeve, but it involves you, and Ned, *off site*, and a lot of danger. I don't want to scare you, but the Heron is up to his neck in this. If we're to catch him, we're going to have to do something between us which is very, *very* risky.' Robyn dropped her voice to a whisper, because walls had ears, even if they were maze walls.

35

'I don't like the idea of you confronting him on your own, Robyn,' Mary said, as she wheeled her bicycle towards the big gates. 'It's not safe – we don't know the half of what he's capable of.'

'And I don't want you and Ned to put yourselves in danger, but I don't know what else we can do,' Robyn said, shrugging.

'Tell someone?' Mary suggested.

'But who can we trust? Not my parents and not Ned's. There's no one here that hasn't lied to us or isn't keeping some kind of secret from us. It's an off-site job, and you and Ned are the only ones who can do it. I'm stuck here, so I might as well make myself useful,' she said as Mary got out her pass, ready to show the sentry guard.

'Promise me you won't try and get into his office?' Mary slung her satchel across her body and mounted her bicycle.

'Sorry, can't. Got to do whatever it takes,' Robyn whispered, hand in front of her mouth. 'Stick to the plan.

Get to the brickyard. You and Ned lie in wait; he'll come because he's a creature of habit, and when he does, you've got to trap him in that tunnel.'

'If we can find the tunnel exit at the brickyard end,' Mary reminded her.

'You'll find it. And then get out of there,' Robyn said, without a smile on her face. This was no laughing matter.

'I'll come and find you in the loft as soon as I can. Don't do anything stupid!' Mary called the last bit over her shoulder, as she cycled towards the hut.

Robyn didn't answer but smiled and waved instead. She didn't want to lie to Mary, but there was no way she was going to leave any stone unturned when it came to the Heron. But first, she had to get past Miss Hughes. That room had to be full of clues, even if the Heron had already cleared his desk.

Inside, the Mansion was bedlam. The building was buzzing with importance and crackling with energy. Robyn knew it had something to do with the arrival of the Americans. She walked as casually as she could past the Heron's office. Miss Hughes gave her an uninterested glance and went back to typing. His door was shut but that didn't mean he was in there. He might well be up in the gallery right now, opening that painting with his traitorous gloved hands. Robyn took the stairs two at a time but the gallery was clear. No sign of him at all.

'Ah, lass! Just the ticket. Joy's been missing you, I reckon,' Mr Samuels said as she walked into the loft.

He was putting back pigeon carriers. He stacked a few

of them neatly before jotting something down in his little notebook. She didn't bother to ask him where he'd been, because he'd tell her if he could. He wasn't a man of mystery or intrigue. He didn't have a hidden agenda and showed no interest in the painting out on the gallery. Mr Samuels was far more interested in the birds than in any other business at Bletchley. Even if Robyn asked him, he'd know nothing about caves or galleries, let alone islands.

He opened his pack-up and held it out to her. She nodded and reached inside for a freshly baked drop scone. There was no butter or jam, but it didn't matter; the scone melted in her mouth.

'Take this over to her and then you can feed the squabs.' Mr Samuels passed her the flask of water.

When she checked on Joy, she was asleep again. The sick pigeon did little else these days. Although she'd never admit it to anyone, every time she left the loft, Robyn said a silent goodbye to Joy, just in case. She gathered up Joy's and Charity's bowls and poured the stale water into one. Balancing carefully, she cracked open the small window and tipped the water out onto the roof. Below, the drive was packed with people trekking across it. Someone whistled. Ladies' heels click-clacked in the distance. A few horns honked, and then, as Robyn watched in horror, Ned's father's hearse pulled up.

The driver's door opened and the Heron stepped out on his stilt-like legs. The water bowl slipped from Robyn's fingers and rolled down the roof, stopping when it hit the guttering. The Heron raised his head at the sound. Robyn ducked and held her breath. Despite her willing it not to, the bowl toppled over the edge and landed on the drive. She heard an almighty smash and couldn't stop herself from jumping up to look out of the window. The driver's door was wide open, and the Heron had disappeared, again. Had he seen her, or the bowl? Was he on his way up the stairs now?

'Did you hear me, lass? I'm away home,' Mr Samuels said. 'Sapped after that journey, and I've another to make.'

He was carrying two travel crates: Charity in one and Faith in the other. 'I'll be back in the morning. You can manage things here, can't you?'

'Yes, no bother,' she said, distracted. 'I'll be fine.'

'If there's anything you need, you know where I am, lass. Or send a message with one of the birds!' he joked.

Robyn fed Joy, even though she'd barely touched her last feed, while she waited for the Heron to steal in and shout at her, or worse, give her the sack and ban her from looking after Joy.

36

When the gallery floorboards rasped, Robyn thought Mr Samuels had forgotten something. She went to open the loft door for him, but saw that it was in fact the Heron. The sight of him made her sick. She held the door ajar. He hadn't come up here for her, of course he hadn't. He was only interested in that painting and the tunnel! Was he about to sneak back to the brickyard already? She'd sent Mary to wait with Ned in the hope that they would catch the Heron in the act. The Heron pressed the frame with his gloved hands and it opened with a click and that familiar huff of air. With his long thin legs, he had no trouble mounting the top rung of the ladder. He was about to descend into the tunnel, when he saw her!

'You!' he spat, almost losing his grip.

Robyn thought about running out and slamming the painting shut in his face, but she was too slow. He unfurled himself, landing back on the gallery. He stalked over to her before she had a chance to run. She'd never get past him now. He grabbed her by both arms and shook her, lifting her off her feet.

'What are you doing?' he hissed in her face.

She'd never seen an adult so angry. She opened her mouth wide to scream but nothing came out.

'What did you see?' he demanded, dragging her over to the tunnel behind the painting. Was he going to throw her down it?

'Everything!' she shouted in his face.

His fingers were digging into her flesh. Pumping her arms, Robyn tried to loosen his vice-like grip.

'Damned idiot! Damn you. Damn it all!' he swore.

When the Heron let go of one of her arms to try to click the lock shut again she took her chance. She stamped on his shiny black shoe and he let go of her other arm. Robyn took a few steps back and then, head down, like a goose before it charges, she ran at him with all her might. The Heron lost his balance and slammed into the wall. As he hit the ground, something fell out of his suit pocket. The tinny echo rang in her ears as she realised the Heron's gun was on the floor. She reached down to pick it up before she had time to process what she was doing. The metal was cold, iron-cold, and as hard as granite. She didn't know how to hold it, so she wrapped both hands around the base and lifted it into the air in front of her.

'Put that down. Put it down, now!' he groaned. There was blood coming from his head. He must have hit the edge of the frame when she shoved him.

'Get up,' she heard herself say.

Amazingly, he did. He listened to her, staggering to his feet, one hand clutching the back of his head.

'Get in there!' She pointed with the gun. It felt like the ice-skin of the lake in the winter when she cracked it for the ducks.

'Are you mad?' He shook his head in disbelief and then laughed at her.

'Don't you dare laugh at me. Get in there. Climb up, go on!' Robyn said. He'd laughed at her one time too many.

'You've no idea what you're doing,' he spat. 'What you're meddling with here.'

'I do! I know what you are. You're a spy! And I'm going to tell everyone.' They'd have to listen once they saw what she'd caught.

'You don't understand. This isn't a game. You're playing with fire. It's not what it looks like,' he babbled, coming towards her. 'You stupid child!'

'Get back! Get away from me, I mean it. Stop or I'll . . . shoot! I know how, my granddad taught me, so don't think I won't,' she said, without a wobble to her voice.

'It's a trap; I've set the bait and we're so close. We're this close to catching the . . .' The Heron held his hand up, pinching the air to show her. 'It's all laid out and if you sabotage our plans, I swear –'

'We've been watching you. You took Mr Knox's files. You're sending messages in code. And you've hidden something in the brickyard. You're a spy. *Codename: Doves*!' She blurted out everything she knew. She had to show him she was in control.

Robyn walked towards the Heron, the gun held out in front of her, no longer shaking. She remembered the way he'd treated Mary. How he'd laughed in her face. How he'd terrified her in the Mansion, that first day with the Secrets Act. All the ways in which he'd humiliated her and belittled her friends.

'You talk about being a patriot and fighting for king and country, but you're the worst sort. You're a traitor. I saw you in the hearse and at the brickyard. Gallery. Caves. Island! I worked it all out.' She couldn't help but brag, even though they hadn't quite solved the last piece of the puzzle.

'All right. So you know. But *Codename: Doves* is a trap, and if you don't put that gun down then you're jeopardising everything we've all worked for. All our portraits lost. *Doves* sold to the enemy and then burned! Picasso's *Girl with a Dove* burned!' He looked desperate now. 'We can't let them destroy our art collection.'

'Sold? Paintings? *Picasso?*' She'd heard the name before.

'Yes! Why else would we be moving them from the castles if they weren't in peril? They've already looted and destroyed millions of pounds worth of art.' He looked confused now.

'What castles?'

'The ones in Wales. This Lowry is coming with me too, and the one in my office. Do you want these precious works of art to fall into the enemy's hands?' He spoke as if he were explaining something very simple to a child. 'We will never see them again. And it's not only paintings. No, it's folios, Shakespeare, sculptures! That's why we've been building all the extra huts. We're using the hearses. And

231

delivery trucks. Taking them to the mountain. I thought you said you knew –'

'I don't know . . .' she started to say, when she heard a voice behind her.

'It's all right, Robyn. I'll take things from here. You've done a wonderful job of catching him in the act, at last.'

She turned around to see that the Bow Tie was right behind her. Fingers reaching out to take the gun from her, thank goodness.

'No! Oh God, no! Run!' the Heron screamed, staggering towards her.

Robyn cried out, frightened, and tried to push him away, but the Bow Tie stepped in front to protect her, accidentally tripping Robyn up. The Bow Tie helped her to her feet and then turned the gun on the Heron who was moving towards them.

'Take a step back, please. That's right. Down the rabbit hole we go.' She gestured to the ladder and the tunnel with the gun. 'Don't worry, Robyn, we'll have this dreadful man locked away in no time.'

'What are you doing?' she asked the Bow Tie.

She wanted the Heron to climb back into the tunnel. Ned and Mary could lock him in at the other end, in the brickyard. But now she wasn't sure. The Heron's face changed; he no longer seemed to care about the blood on his head and he wasn't angry with her. He was making his eyes wide and trying to tip his head. It was as if he were telling her silently to run again. The Bow Tie was now standing right in front of him, the gun pressed to his heart.

'Get in,' she ordered, 'Or shall I turn this gun on her – *the*

Lewis girl?' the Bow Tie asked sweetly, without turning around to look at her. 'Bit of a thorn in your side, isn't she!'

'*Me?*' Robyn gaped. 'What?'

'Ah, Robyn, little bird, you've been singing the wrong song. Gallery. Caves. Island – Winston's words, coded in Welsh. And you thought you were so clever, translating them from your mother's tongue: *Ogofâu. Oriel. Ynys.* But you've got the wrong man. You should have looked for the right woman!' She cackled; a sound Robyn had never heard come from the Bow Tie before.

'All that bara brith and those Welsh cakes your mother dropped off at the cottage were worth the added pounds. I had to listen to endless conversations about her beloved Wales!' The Bow Tie smiled slyly. '*Diolch yn fawr*, Mrs Lewis, thank you for the crash course in Welsh.'

'But . . . my mother trusted you. *I* trusted you!' Robyn protested, uncomprehending. 'I thought, *we thought*, you were –'

'Doves in the hearse, is it?' The Bow Tie spun back around to the Heron, completely ignoring Robyn. 'Or at the brickyard, ready for a railway getaway?' She hit his head hard with the butt of the gun.

'Hearse,' the Heron spluttered.

Robyn tried to get to her feet, but her ankle hurt. She didn't think it was broken but she must have landed awkwardly when the Bow Tie tripped her up. Tripped her up? Could she really have done that? Had they truly got the Heron all wrong?

'Keys?' The Bow Tie kicked his leg hard with the toe of her shoe.

'In the ignition,' the Heron said, wincing.

'You have made this easy for me. Get up!' She laughed, pushing the gun into his temple so that the Heron groaned. Blood trailed down the back of his jacket as he began to pull himself up towards the ladder.

'That's it. And I'll take those, thank you,' the Bow Tie said, carefully pulling off the brown leather gloves and setting them on the floor.

The Bow Tie waited until the Heron was ready to climb down the ladder. With the gun in one hand, she swung the big painting shut with the other. It slammed onto the Heron's bony fingers, which had been holding onto the top rung. The Heron screamed as the Bow Tie casually slipped the gloves on and clicked the painting shut.

Robyn's mind raced. How could she have got it all so wrong? This was all her fault, because if anything happened to the Heron, if he fell from the ladder, or his fingers were broken or . . . or he died, it would be because of her. All of this was her fault.

'I've wanted to do that for some time. We both have, haven't we? We've a lot in common. We are great at people watching. Listening at doors. Picking up the scraps and gobbling them down, like your rats in there.' She nodded at the pigeon loft.

'No! You leave my Joy alone!' Robyn shouted, dragging herself up off the floor.

She wanted to run but couldn't put any weight on her foot.

'Oh, I'm not interested in your flea-ridden pigeons, not when there's doves to be had. Did you know, pigeon in

French means "peeping chick"? Rather like you and your spying friends. Easily duped. Not like the dove; such a beautiful bird. Symbolising peace and freedom, which is just what the prize down in that hearse will bring me. Peace and freedom in the form of Picasso's *Girl with a Dove*. And the rest of them, of course. Da Vinci, Botticelli's *Mother and Child*, a Van Gogh, some Rembrandts. And Turner, of course; how terribly British. All hidden in the brickyard, waiting to be loaded up onto the freight train. And then off to your mother's land.' The Bow Tie laughed, seeing her face.

'Wales?' Robyn checked.

'That's right. And there's a lovely Shakespeare folio too. What an unexpected bonus! I thought it was ruined when the National Gallery was bombed. I can't imagine a cold damp quarry is a good hiding place for priceless works of art. But no matter now, it's not as if they'll ever make it to Wales.'

'But why are the paintings going to Wales?'

'Not as bright as you would like to think, are you, Robyn? Not like your clever friend, Mary. Had to keep her terribly busy with puzzles and jobs, so that she left me alone to do mine!' The Bow Tie stepped towards her and pulled her up sharply by her elbow.

'Here, let me help you, poor thing.' She wrapped her arm around Robyn's shoulder, guiding her firmly towards the loft door.

'You tricked us? You lied to us!' she accused. 'I . . . I admired you, looked up to you. I *liked* you.'

'Smells like a stable in here.' The Bow Tie wrinkled her

nose in disgust, ignoring Robyn entirely. 'And so do you!' The Bow Tie shoved her to the floor.

'What's wrong with you? How could you? Why are you doing this?' she demanded.

'For the money, of course. It's always about the money. Do you think I want to spend the rest of my life on a paltry Foreign Office salary? Do you know what they pay the men here? I do a better job than most of them, with no recognition. No doubt I'll be demoted to a secretary in some dusty old office after the war. Or worse, *married*! No, thank you!' The Bow Tie shook her head then scanned the room. Her eyes settled on the black telephone set.

She tucked the gun into the waistband of her skirt and assessed Robyn again.

'What are you doing?' Robyn asked uncertainly, terrified by this woman who was now a stranger.

'Hand me your penknife. Don't pretend you don't have it. I've had to put up with you droning on, showing me every single function and feature of that blasted thing. Like it was the crown jewels. Hand it over, now.' She held out her hand.

Robyn reached into one of the pockets of her overalls and pulled out her grandfather's penknife. The Bow Tie snatched it up, dashed over to the telephone and cut the wires.

'There now, that'll do nicely,' she said, replacing the now-useless receiver with care.

'You promised. You signed the Official Secrets Act,' Robyn reminded her.

'I did, and I meant it, but I've been overlooked repeatedly. Not *man* enough for the job, when I could do it standing

236

on my head. And when a better offer came along, I'd have been a fool to turn it down. You'll understand when you grow up. When you're a woman too.' The Bow Tie almost looked sorry for a second before carrying on.

'"Not one picture shall leave this island. Hide them in caves and cellars if you must," Mr Churchill said. Well, there's no need for that, is there, dear prime minister? No need for any pictures to leave this island, not when there's a lovely big kiln at the brickyard. Couldn't have made it any easier for me, could they? Popping that tunnel exit right by the kiln, how thoughtful,' she said, undoing her bow tie.

She shook it until it hung loosely around her neck. A key fell from the material and the Bow Tie caught it in her hand.

'What are you doing? There's still time to change your mind, you could . . . stay here and talk to me?' Robyn pleaded, thinking of Ned, Mary and Ned's mother, Helen, at the brickyard.

They had no idea about who the Bow Tie actually was. Nor what she was capable of with the Heron's gun in her possession.

'Time for the doves to fly right up that flaming chimney and into the sky!' The Bow Tie smiled, ignoring Robyn yet again.

The Bow Tie took one last look around the loft. She nodded with satisfaction at Robyn lying on the floor. Her swollen ankle was already blooming blue and yellow with bruises. Then, the Bow Tie walked through the door, the polka-dot bow tie falling to the ground next to her. The loft door slammed shut. The key turned in the lock, followed by the sound of heels clip-clopping down the Mansion stairs.

37

'What am I going to do?' Robyn asked the empty loft. 'What should I do?' she called out to the vacant space. 'I've been such an idiot. *How* could I have been so stupid? She said she'd duped us, tricked us, right from the start. She was under my nose. Staring me in the face but I didn't see it.'

She hefted herself up into a sitting position and pushed off the floor with both hands, then cried out in pain as she tried to balance on her sore ankle. It was no good. Even if she could have dragged herself to the telephone, the Bow Tie had already seen to it.

'Help? Help! Hello? Anyone?' she cried out over the clatter of typewriters and teleprinters downstairs.

Robyn looked up at the windows for a moment, wondering, but knew it was no good. She could fit a shoulder and her head through one of the gaps, but not her whole body. Not after the growth spurt she'd had since she started working as an apprentice. Besides, the driveway was empty so there was no one to call to anyway.

'Think, Robyn, think!' she told herself, twisting and turning to look at every single item in the loft. Her trusty *What to Do in Any Wartime Emergency* booklet didn't have a handy guide to getting out of this situation.

There had to be something she could use to escape. Her penknife might have helped. She could have tried to pick the lock. But the Bow Tie had pocketed it – her mother would be furious. Mr Samuels had taken his toolkit with him, along with the best pigeons. He wouldn't be back until tomorrow morning. She could last in here until then, she wasn't worried about that, but she had to stop the Bow Tie from burning doves. And all the other works of art! She had to warn her friends. Ned and Mary would try to stop the Bow Tie when they realised what she was up to. If anything happened to them, or Ned's mother, if that woman . . . she would never ever forgive herself.

'Stop. Just stop. Calm down. Think!'

Robyn was panicked, desperate and could hardly breathe. She looked around for the flask of water, hoping there'd be some left. As she reached across to weigh the flask and check the contents, she knocked a box of green capsules over. The sound made Joy stir in her crate.

'Sshhh, it's all right. I won't let any harm come to you,' Robyn promised, opening the cage to see if Joy would come to her. It might calm her down.

She held out her hand and the pigeon tentatively stepped onto it. Joy looked at her, eyes brighter than they'd been in days. Robyn stroked Joy's soft, warm head and tried to slow her breathing. Joy made soft snuffling sounds, searching for feed; she must be hungry at last! Robyn pulled out a packet and poured some into her hand for the pigeon to peck. On seeing their mother, Dilly and Alice started making a racket in their hutches. Eager and confident, their movements reminded her of Joy in her prime. Robyn popped Joy back in the crate but left the door open. She bent down and picked up the green capsules. When she turned back round to put them in the box, Joy had disappeared.

'Joy? Joy!' Robyn called, looking around the loft desperately.

The sound came from above, a cooing and shuffling on the beams. Joy had flown a little way up, above Robyn's head, settling in the eaves. Just as she had the first time the Heron barged into the loft and scared them all. Oh God, the Heron! He was still in the tunnel! And even if he made it to the brickyard exit, Ned and Mary would have blocked it. He'd be trapped in there and he wouldn't be able to stop the Bow Tie and it was all her fault. She started sobbing, feeling hopeless.

'Oh, Joy. Why didn't I stop and listen to him?' she asked the bird who was now pecking at her clenched fist. 'I always think I know best. When will I learn?'

She opened her fist, thinking Joy wanted food, but she was holding the green capsule, not corn.

'No. I can't. Can I? You can't, can you?' Robyn thought aloud.

Would Joy be able to fly? And even if she could, where would Robyn send her? And who to? What would she say? She didn't have the right kind of paper to put in the capsule. Or a pen. Robyn patted the pockets of her overalls. She was feeling for something when her hand settled on the booklet: *What to Do in Any Wartime Emergency*.

'If ever there was an emergency, this is it, Joy!' she told the pigeon as she opened the booklet and ripped out one of the small, flimsy pages.

She tapped her other pocket and found a stubby little pencil. She licked it to moisten it; it could do with sharpening but there wasn't time now.

'What can I even write? Even if I can fit this in there and you can take it and . . . never mind. Write something!'

She'd have to write like the telegrams she'd seen coming into the park, with all their full stops. She looked down at the ground searching for the right words and saw the spotty tie. She picked it up and placed it next to the paper. *Doves. Brickyard. Bow Tie. Traitor.*

Mrs Ashman wouldn't be giving her a certificate for penmanship, but it was at least legible. She rolled up the message and inserted it into the capsule. Joy tilted her head, watching. Robyn could have sworn the pigeon understood the importance of this mission. That was what this was, a real mission. Robyn picked up the bow tie and placed it around Joy's neck. She made sure it was knotted securely so that it wouldn't come loose.

'Joy. Fly home,' she said, attaching the capsule to Joy's leg.

Joy would understand and remember her first home, Mr Samuels' house, where she had been reared as a squab. It had been her first homing instinct, and pigeons, the best of birds, could have more than one home. Besides, Joy was already in Bletchley Park so there was only one other place she knew to return to. Robyn had to pray that the memory was still there, and that Joy would be able to travel the short distance. A stone's throw, Mr Samuels had said. Joy just had to deliver the message and make it through her last-ever mission, safely.

38

October 1940

Mr Samuels was talking to a stout man in a crisp white shirt. He was wearing a black waistcoat and smart pinstriped trousers, and he looked familiar. As Robyn entered the loft, they both turned around . . . and her mouth fell open and she dropped her sketch book on the floor. The Heron had grudgingly returned it, so she could stop drawing on the backs of envelopes.

'I was most sorry to hear of the loss of your pigeon,' said the visitor. 'Her bravery knows no bounds. You have both my admiration and thanks.'

'Oh,' Robyn managed, picking up her sketch book.

'These animals hold in their hearts the very spirit of our resistance. We will remember the fallen. I'd like to present you with this award for Joy,'

The man passed Mr Samuels a medal and a piece of paper. 'Thank you, sir,' Mr Samuels said. 'That's most kind.' Robyn could see his eyes filling with tears as he handed the medal to her.

Robyn said nothing. Joy had completed her final mission, reaching Mr Samuels in time. The Bow Tie was stopped, before she could do damage to either *Doves* or Ned and Mary. Robyn had got the Heron completely wrong, she acknowledged as he entered the loft.

Perhaps it was the emotion, or the relief – Robyn dropped a curtsey to Winston Churchill, the prime minister of Great Britain. The Heron snorted with laughter. Even if he wasn't the guilty party they'd thought, he was still the rudest man she'd ever met. At least he'd never receive a medal like Joy's, she thought happily. It was, after all, a carrier pigeon, the best of birds, who had saved the day, not the Heron.

'You may leave us. Come back and collect me in ten minutes,' Mr Churchill told the Heron crisply.

The Heron didn't make eye contact with Robyn but turned on the heel of his shiny shoe and limped off out of the loft, leaning on his stick. Since the incident in the tunnel, he'd stayed on the ground floor, as he hadn't been able to manage the stairs, although he seemed to have made an exception today. She couldn't help remembering the folk tale she'd told Mary about the wren and how if you harmed one, it'd bring you bad luck, in the form of a broken leg! Of course, it was the Bow Tie who permanently damaged the Heron's leg, when she pushed him down the tunnel. Robyn had tried to apologise to him, several times in fact. He waved away her apologies; she wasn't sure if it was forgiveness as such, but he didn't seem angry with her any more. She stood up straight, grateful that Mr Churchill hadn't laughed at her. She knew Mr Samuels *never* would. What had she been thinking, curtseying like that?

'I thought you might like to show Mr Churchill around, lass. While he's got five minutes' peace from his schedule,' Mr Samuels suggested.

Robyn showed the prime minister the hutches, the remaining birds and the landing platform. She explained how the bell worked, showed him Mr Samuels' logbook and the systems he had put in place. All the while, she looked to Mr Samuels to see if she was doing the right thing. He gave her small nods of encouragement as she brought Mr Churchill back to the squabs.

'And these are Joy's squabs. I've been looking after them. There's two, see, but I think this one is the champion. She's called Dilly.'

Mr Churchill exchanged the swiftest of looks with Mr Samuels. It was a relief to Robyn to know that she, Mary and Ned had cleared Mr Knox's name, now the Bow Tie was under arrest.

'And the other one, Alice, she's not going to be a carrier pigeon because of her foot. See, she's got pigeonpox, which I think just makes her special.' She showed Mr Churchill the damage. 'Mr Samuels says birds manage and get on with it and it's just us humans who make a fuss about such things . . . I wonder, Mr Samuels, do you think I could make a gift of Alice?'

'She's been in your care, lass,' Mr Samuels said. 'You know what's best for her.'

'Although Alice will fly well, despite her foot, she'll never be a working carrier pigeon. And if she isn't going to follow in her mother's footsteps, then Bletchley Park might not be the best place for her, sir.'

Both men nodded and waited for her to continue. She took a deep breath.

'Mr Churchill, do you think that Princess Elizabeth would like another pet? I've read in my father's newspaper that she loves her horses and dogs. And am I right in thinking that her family are fond of birds too? Pigeons especially? You see, this one, Alice, is a special bird after all, but she can't stay here.' Robyn was thinking on her feet.

Mr Churchill said, turning to her, 'She would be most delighted. Mr Samuels, can you see to it that this remarkable gift reaches Princess Elizabeth? I wonder, are you of a similar age?' He tilted his head to consider her.

'Yes, we are! In fact, we're the exact same age, fourteen.' Robyn's birthday had come and gone without much fuss and bother; a birthday seemed to matter less this year, after everything she'd been through. 'Although the princess's birthday is in April and I've only just had mine, so, technically she's older. But she lives at BP and so do I!' she said, delighted. 'We have *so* much in common.'

'BP – do you know, I'd never made the connection before. You *are* a bright young thing,' Mr Churchill said, and for the first time she blushed, just a little.

'I've named my favourite chickens Lilibet and

Margaret-Rose, after the princesses. It might be better not to tell them that,' Robyn added.

'It will be our secret, as shall my visit here.' Mr Churchill tapped his nose. 'I'm sure Princess Elizabeth will send you a thank-you note; she has truly little company, currently, and for the foreseeable future, I'm afraid. She may welcome a pen pal. I am of course unable to share your address with her, here at the park, but the correspondence will reach you safely. Perhaps you could send her some of those drawings?' He pointed to some of the doodles she'd drawn of Joy and her squabs on the scraps of mail Mary had saved for her; they'd fallen out of her sketch book, but she hadn't noticed.

She bent down and was going to stuff them in the back of the book when Mr Churchill held out his hand.

'Now then . . .' he said, pushing his round spectacles further up his nose; he looked a little like an owl, she thought, and wondered what he'd be like to sketch. She did prefer animals overall, but his face was interesting, to say the least.

'Ah, I see you are an artist. I like to think of myself as something of a dabbler, although there are plenty who would disagree. But you and I know full well, beauty is in the eye of the beholder. A fine work of art is worth its weight in gold. Keep up the excellent work, miss.' And then he carefully handed back her sketches and tipped the brow of his hat to her.

He nodded at Mr Samuels. 'Will you see me out, Alfred?'

Mr Churchill left the loft, as if his presence were an everyday occurrence. The loft door shut but swung open again due to the breeze from the windows. The men's voices floated back in.

'Quite the place you have here, Alfred.'

'Aye, it is. We have clever people, carrier pigeons and the machine itself!' Mr Samuels agreed.

'And a *secretum cuniculum* too,' Mr Churchill sounded impressed. 'You all look so innocent. One would never think that there was such secrecy here. But a picture, or in our case a portrait, is worth a thousand words.'

Secretum cuniculum – what did that mean?

'What will happen to her now?' Mr Samuels asked.

They could only be talking about one person: the Bow Tie!

'She'll be given the choice to work for British Intelligence or face execution. The Double-Cross System is exceptionally good at turning spies. Of course, she already comes equipped with her own gadgets. Quick thinking on the young girl's part to pop the tie on the pigeon. Admirable. I'll see to it that she gets some new paints, pencils and paper; quite the young artist in the making. But it doesn't do for her to draw on the back of mail and messages – you never know what might still be hidden inside. Speaking of which, that bow tie was an excellent hiding place for messages composed in microdots; it's quite put me off wearing my own –'

'Ready, sir? The train is waiting,' she heard the Heron cut in.

'Travel safely, sir. Until next time,' Mr Samuels said.

'Thank you, Alfred. I'll see to it that you have all you want, on extreme priority. You helped me keep my promise. I did say, not one painting shall leave this island, even if we have to hide them in caves and cellars. None must go. We will beat them! Although I hadn't expected a hearse and a brave pigeon to be part of the plan, of course!'

When Mr Samuels came back into the loft there was a smile on his face; the first one she'd seen since Joy died.

'I just met the prime minister!' Robyn exclaimed.

'Aye, lass, and you'll not forget it, likely,' he said, smiling at her.

'But how did he get into Bletchley without everyone noticing?'

'Well, those in the know *knew*. They timed the machines to stop as he walked into one of the huts and to start up all at the same time as he left! Word spread and there was a right old crowd gathered outside by the time he came out. He had to give them a few words. As you know, lass, he likes to talk.'

Mr Samuels had technically answered her question, but she still felt as if he'd diverted her somehow.

'What did he say?' she asked, wondering if either of her parents had been there to hear him.

'Well, now, quite a lot, as it happens. Let me see what I can recall,' Mr Samuels teased. 'He thanked the staff for the part they played during . . . *various operations*. Then stole away up here to say hello and to see what's what with the National Pigeon Service.'

'But how do you know him?' Robyn dared to ask. She wasn't sure that she liked Mr Churchill. Although he was of course impressive. She wondered how these two quite different men knew each other.

'The world, as you'll see once you leave the park, is a small place,' Mr Samuels said cautiously.

'To think that Princess Elizabeth might write to me! *To me*!' She could not believe it. Maybe they'd become pen pals and compare notes about Dilly and Alice. She wouldn't believe it until she had the thank-you note in her hand. She'd keep it until she was old and grey, and living a world away from Bletchley Park.

Epilogue

January 1941

Today Ned would officially become a staff member at Bletchley Park: an apprentice in the gardens, working with Noah and Kitty.

Last week, as soon as he'd turned fourteen, Ned had told his father that he didn't want to be an undertaker. Of course, Mr Letton was no longer speaking to him, but his mother had put her foot down and stood up to her husband, so Ned could choose his own path. Ned said his mother had changed since she started working down the brick factory. She went out with the girls now, and people telephoned asking to speak to Helen rather than Mrs Letton. Things were exciting at home after being involved in *Codename: Doves* and the operation in Wales. Ned said the best part was having a secret, just between him and his mother.

Although it was killing her to not be a part of it, Robyn was happy for Ned. And she was excited for herself too, because Ned would be here at the park with her every single day! Happily, Mr Letton had left to resume his duties in the funeral parlour. This meant the children were free to do as they wished, at least during their lunchbreak. Robyn was glad to see the back of the hearse. May it never drive through the gates to the park ever again! Even if it had saved a precious Picasso painting: *Girl with a Dove*, also known as *Girl with a Pigeon*, according to Mr Samuels. Robyn knew which title she preferred. It was odd to think of all those famous paintings hiding in wooden huts and boxes, down a mine somewhere in Wales. She wondered if they would ever make it back to the gallery in London. She wanted to see the Picasso for herself, one day.

She and Ned had the most exciting plan for their lunchbreak today. That afternoon, Dilly was setting off on her first solo mission as a Bletchley Park carrier pigeon. But first, there was Mary's letter to read again. Robyn and Ned had bicycled to the edge of the park, far away from the pigeon lofts at the top of the Mansion. This was the furthest Robyn could go without breaking the rules, and after everything that had happened recently, she was willing to follow the rules, for now. They settled down on the ground and Ned drew out Mary's letter from the pocket of his overalls.

'How did Mary know your address?' she asked, as Ned passed it to her.

'She looked up Letton and Sons in the telephone directory,' Ned explained.

Clever Mary.

'Easier than trying to get it past the censors here,' Ned agreed.

Robyn suspected the letter would be the first of many, as Mary was an excellent correspondent. She and Ned, however, were not. Writing letters was hard work. Mary's looked like it might be even harder work to read, thrilled as they'd initially been to receive word from her.

Dearest Carroll

All is well. The bright young things and I are learning languages together. We're all mad here, speaking in tongues – secretum cuniculum. What a strange world we live in, but it is no use going back to yesterday, I was a different person then.

I was told that if I pass my next set of exams (I was top of the class last week!) they might invite me back into Wonderland, although not on a bicycle but in a boat – keeping it in the family. Aye, aye, captain. It's a case of wren not when; we'll be birds of a feather, Robyn.

Your Alice x

'She's going to join the Wrens! Her father will be so pleased,' Ned said with a sigh.

'Your father will come round. One day,' Robyn promised, hoping.

'She sounds happy,' Ned said. 'I always knew being a boffin would pay off for Mary. But give me a spade and

253

a wheelbarrow any day! 1941 is going to be *my* year,' he decided. 'I've got a good feeling.'

The Heron, who, it turned out, wasn't *quite* the worst of sorts, had found Mary a place in a special school where people were being taught Italian and maybe other languages too. Mary had practically ripped the rail pass and accommodation permit out of his hand.

'Do you think she'll come back, here, to us?' Ned asked, tucking the letter back into one of his pockets.

'It sounds like it. You know Mary. She's bound to pass her exams with flying colours. *Flying* – do you get it? The Wrens!

'That's a terrible joke, Robyn, even for you. Anyway, what exams do you think they're making her do?' Ned wondered.

'Languages, I expect. It sounds to me like she's going to be learning more than one language; she says they're speaking in tongues. I 'spect she'll be translating letters and all that too, she'll be brilliant at it. Did I tell you Joy got a medal for bravery?' She was so proud of Joy.

It still hurt to say her name aloud. And of course, she couldn't tell Ned that Mr Churchill delivered the medal, even though she was desperate to show off.

'She deserves it,' Ned said.

'So, you see, you have quite the legacy to live up to,' Robyn told Dilly, getting to her feet and opening the crate.

She held Dilly by her feet and set her down on the ground, then checked the capsule one last time, securing it correctly. This one didn't have anything important in it, not like Joy's last flight. Today was a test run, just a little fly about

Bletchley. But next time, Dilly would be driven somewhere by Mr Knox and she and some paratrooper would land in another country and, when she flew home, Dilly would be carrying a real message back to the park, from behind enemy lines. Hundreds or even thousands of people's lives would be depending on her, on them.

'Is she ready?' Ned asked, holding up his crossed fingers.

'I think so,' Robyn said, keeping her eyes on Dilly.

'Are *you* ready?' Ned laughed. 'Ready to race her back to the loft?'

'Yes. Although I hope we don't beat her. That wouldn't bode well for her career, would it? Now, Dilly, pep talk time. Your mother was quite the star, one of our finest.'

'She completely saved the day! Just like my mum.' Ned said proudly.

'And I know you aren't going to win us the war all by yourself, but you are going to play your part.' She paused to stroke Dilly's head, still holding onto her feet.

'We all will,' Ned said.

'Because it's not over yet, is it?' she said.

'Not *just* yet,' Ned agreed, with a frown.

'Well, it can't last forever,' Robyn reasoned.

'That's true.' Ned smiled.

'Now, Ned, I'm going to say something from the Bible and you're not to laugh or make fun of me. All right?' She held her hand out.

'All right. And then we run,' Ned agreed, warming up by jogging on the spot, as if he were an Olympic athlete about to compete.

'And then we run,' Robyn agreed before clearing her throat, 'A bird of the air shall carry the voice and that which hath wings shall tell the matter,' she whispered to Dilly.

Then Robyn finally let go of the bird. And with a bob of her head, Dilly took to the clear blue skies over Bletchley Park.

Author's Note

I first visited Bletchley Park on a school trip with my daughter, Evie. I knew it was a special place because we had recently found out that my great-aunt Audrey worked there during the Second World War. She signed the Official Secrets Act at the age of seventeen, and kept the secret for decades, not even telling her husband or children; the document she signed applied not just during wartime but forever. Like most of my family, Audrey had a flair for drama and loved a good story. However she was not forthcoming with details, and we only learned snippets about her time at Bletchley, when she occasionally let her guard down. One of the most exciting things she shared was that after the war she was secretly recruited by . . . but that's a story for another time.

Bletchley Park was one of the most secret places in Britain during the war and is a place I find myself returning to, finding something different each time I visit: a new exhibition, a recent discovery, an unexpected tour guide with a unique story to share or even a celebrity – Bletchley has so many of them. In the early days of the war the total staff numbers at the park were in the hundreds, but the success of the codebreaking effort was phenomenal, and those numbers grew to around 10,000 in 1944; most of the staff were women. There are so many famous people associated with Bletchley: Alan Turing, mathematician, logician, cryptanalyst, designer of the bombe (an electro-mechanical device used by

British cryptologists to help decipher German machine-encrypted secret messages), head of Hut 8 and pioneering computer scientist; Ian Fleming, the James Bond novelist; Valerie Glassborow, grandmother of the Princess of Wales; Betty Webb, codebreaker, recently awarded the Legion d'Honneur; Commander Alastair Denniston, head of the Government Code and Cypher School; Dilly Knox, leading cryptologist, who cracked the code of the commercial Enigma machines; Dilly's Fillies: Joan Clarke; Mavis Batey, Margaret Rock, and so many more. Although I may have played around with dates a little, to suit my story, it is true that Winston Churchill, then prime minister, once paid a secret visit, and so did King George VI. And Bletchley was in fact bombed in November 1940, although the railway was most likely the target, rather than the park itself.

We now know much more about Churchill's orders to move priceless works of art from the National Gallery in London, to Manod, in North Wales, and it was during a Bletchley Park podcast that I discovered some of the nation's masterpieces had come by train, through Bletchley, to the brick yard. But it's all the things we don't know about the people who slipped back into their private lives, once the war was over, that fascinate me. Here lie the best stories, just out of our reach behind the 'roped off areas', lurking in undiscovered files, or whispered in someone's ear decades later. The success of Bletchley's codebreakers in breaking the German cypher systems Enigma and Lorenz are credited with shortening the war by two years. I can only begin to imagine what it must have felt like, never being able to tell anybody the part you played, because you had been sworn to secrecy. I'm not sure we'd be able to keep such a secret today.

It's quite likely that at some point, you might find yourself on a school trip to Bletchley, or perhaps you'll visit with friends and family. If you do, go, and find Robyn's cottage, or Joy's loft, and be highly suspicious of any paintings, because you never know what might be lurking behind them. And, if you have time, seek out the Commemorative Codebreakers' Wall and try to spy my great-aunt's brick. Here is a clue to help you:

Acknowledgements

I owe a debt of gratitude to my wonderful agent, Gillie Russell, who believed in this story from the start and never once doubted my ability to tell it, speaking about my characters as if they were waiting for us in the next room. Such an agent is truly a gift. Thank you, Gillie, I could not have done it without you.

Endless thanks to my first readers, Mum and Evie, who both read and reread countless versions of the manuscript. 10/10 to Evie for your hawk-eye editorial skills – you deserve a pay rise. Noah, thanks for listening to me read out chapters in coffee shops. Joe, you humoured me each time I told you the latest 'fascinating' fact about pigeons, even though you weren't remotely interested. Thank you, Dad, for reading this story in record time and not guessing the plot twist. Thank you, Aunty Pat (Ashman), for sharing the details of your mum's extraordinary story with me and for encouraging me to write this book. Diolch yn fawr.

Every member of staff I met at Bletchley Park was kind enough to help me with my research, even during lockdown when the doors closed to the public. Special thanks to Peronel Craddock, Head of Programmes at Bletchley Park Trust, and Thomas Cheetham, research officer at Bletchley Park Trust. Arts Council England kindly awarded me a grant to write this book, which was an honour, as well as enormously helpful financially. I am most grateful to Pete Stones for the support offered, during and after the application process. Thank you, Emma Pass – your wise words helped me find the key to unlock a particularly stubborn subplot. Biggest cwtches to Eloise Williams – you keep me going with our daily chats and your steadfast belief in me as a writer. I hope you know the feeling is mutual. Emma Carroll is one of the most generous writers I've had the pleasure to meet, and if you've not already discovered her books you're in for a treat – thank you for loving my book as much as I've loved yours, Emma.

Of course it is a myth that anyone writes a book alone. There is, if you are lucky, a supportive team behind every word. I was and am delighted (still pinching myself!) that editor extraordinaire Ruth Bennett fell in love with Robyn, Ned and Mary, editing their story with heart and humour and great insight. I appreciate copy editors Talya Baker and Anna Bowles, who not only saved me from many mistakes but made the text better each time they worked on it. Thank you to the whole team at Piccadilly Press for the time and effort you have spent on this book.

The first time I saw David Dean's cover for I, Spy, I gasped in *the* most melodramatic way; thank you, David, for capturing the characters and the heart and soul of I, Spy so accurately and authentically.

Libraries have always been a special place for me, a sanctuary of sorts, and I can't wait to see I, Spy being borrowed. Thank you to all the librarians, booksellers and teachers who introduced me to books and who continue to share a love of reading with future generations.

And finally, thanks to you, reader-with-most-excellent taste, for choosing this book. May it prove worthy of your time.

About the Author

Rhian Tracey was born in Swansea and grew up on the Welsh borders. She got her first publishing deal at twenty-six. Rhian teaches several days a week in an SEN department, working with students who have dyslexia, dyspraxia, autism, ADD and other additional learning needs. She also volunteers with Medical Detection Dogs, helping to train puppies who will go on to be assistance dogs. Rhian lives in Northamptonshire with her children and dog.